MYSTERIES OF MICHIGAMI

by Enid Cleaves

"Mysteries of Michigami," by Enid Cleaves. ISBN 978-1-62137-240-0.

Published 2013 by Virtualbookworm.com Publishing Inc., P.O. Box 9949, College Station, TX 77842, US. ©2013, Enid Cleaves. All rights reserved. No part of this publication may be reproduced, stored in a retrieval system, or transmitted in any form or by any means, electronic, mechanical, recording or otherwise, without the prior written permission of Enid Cleaves.

Manufactured in the United States of America.

INTRODUCTION

In my book, *Ghostly Tales of Lake Superior,* I wrote of personal experiences that I could not explain: a music box that suddenly started to play after many months of neglect, sounds of muffled voices at night, and many other strange events that occurred at our home in Northern Wisconsin. I am still waiting to see an apparition, or maybe to have a psychic experience—many of my friends and acquaintances have related incidents that they have experienced. Perhaps I am looking too hard—in all the wrong places! Speaking of looking in the wrong places...all four pair of my reading glasses have disappeared. Maybe Paul is at work again (Paul Tergeist)—our resident spirit!

The above-mentioned book told of legends, haunted places, and strange happenings around Lake Superior. *Mysteries of Michigami* covers stories around Lake Michigan, called *Michigami* (great waters) by the Algonquin people who inhabited its shores. The lake is much more populated around its 1,600 miles of shoreline than Lake Superior. Large cities such as Chicago, Milwaukee, Gary, and Green Bay give the lake a metropolitan atmosphere, as opposed to the wild and forested Lake Superior. Michigami is third largest Great Lake, and the only one entirely within the United States. It is over 300 miles long (depending on what encyclopedia you consult) and 118 miles across at its widest stretch. Michigami has an area of 22,400 square miles. It averages 279 feet in depth and is 925 feet at its deepest point. It is one of four of the Great Lakes bordering the state of Michigan. In fact, if you travel from *anywhere* in Michigan, it is no further than 85 miles to one of the four: Superior, Michigan, Huron or Erie! The Lake does not face the "gales of

November" that Superior experiences; nevertheless, an estimated 10,000 vessels have gone down here, with approximately 30,000 lost lives.

Lake Michigan has a beauty of its own, with stately lighthouses, secluded harbors, rocky cliffs and sandy dunes. It has its share of stories too: Some about ghosts and lake monsters, but others of a different nature: like gangsters and werewolves. This book is too short to cover all of the haunted places and mysterious happenings that have occurred in and around the Lake, but it contains a variety of stories. In a few instances, names have been changed because of the wishes of the individuals or to maintain the privacy of the family or descendants of the protagonist. Enjoy the tales; I've enjoyed experiencing the search for them!

DEDICATION

My mother (Millie) and my husband (Bob) accompanied me on a trip across Lake Michigan via the Manitowoc-Ludington car-ferry. We drove north along the eastern shore of the Lake, visiting places like Sleeping Dunes State Park before winding our way back to northern Wisconsin through the Upper Peninsula. Mom would come along on many trail walks. If the stroll turned out to be a bit of a climb, we would take our time and push and pull her up the hill or steps as necessary! She always loved to go on "trips," to explore, to see different places.

Mom passed away in the summer of 2004 at age 88 from complications caused by a broken hip. She fell while crossing a cement driveway near the assisted living home in Iola, Wisconsin where she had resided for a little over a year. She always enjoyed walking, and was on a short jaunt down the block from her residence when she fell. On the first anniversary of her death, a gladiola opened its pure white petals on one of the perennials I had transplanted from Mom's garden. It was the only one that bloomed that summer.

Bob passed away in December 2010. Despite constant health issues, he was always willing to accompany me on my travels and search for stories and legends. Without him I know that I would not have made nearly as many visits to the lighthouses, mansions, inns, and places that held tales of ghosts and strange occurrences. Bob guest-authored a chapter in this book: "Blood Moon Rising." This, and other of his writings, grew from the ability to imagine and relate the fantasy world that existed within his own mind. He often declared that he lived in "Middle Earth."

Mom, I know that your spirit was with us in later travels. When your stride became slower and shorter as the trail got steeper, you were hanging tighter to our belts. "As the going gets tough, the tough get going." And you were one tough lady!

Bob, thanks for coming along, even if was only "to carry my bags" as you joked to our friends. I know that you had a good time too! I miss our travels together.

CONTENTS

CHAPTER 1: IF MEN WERE WOLVES
....1

CHAPTER 2: WHO'S APPEARING AT THE BIOGRAPH
....9

CHAPTER 3: MARY STILL TARRIES
....25

CHAPTER 4: GULLIVER'S GHOULS AND BUOYS
....33

CHAPTER 5: THE KEY TO ROOM 310
....45

CHAPTER 6: EDYE'S DREAMS
....59

CHAPTER 7: LET SLEEPING BEARS LIE
....65

CHAPTER 8: SNAKES IN THE WAKE
....71

CHAPTER 9: GHOSTS HAVE FUN IN CHESTERTON
....75

CHAPTER 10: BLOOD MOON RISING
....83

CHAPTER 11: SCALENE SCENE
....98

CHAPTER 12: SPIRITS WITH A WHITE CAST
....107

CHAPTER 13: THE HAUNTED FARMHOUSE
....119

CHAPTER 14: DOGMAN DOGMA
....123

CHAPTER 15: DON'T GIVE UP THE GHOST
....131

SELECTED BIBLIOGRAPHY
.. ..I

CHAPTER 1

IF MEN WERE WOLVES

**Even a man who is pure in heart
And says his prayers by night,
May become a wolf when the wolf-bane blooms,
And the autumn moon is bright.[1]**

Where in the world would a werewolf wander, if a moonstruck monster might meander? Maybe in the Midwest! At least, that is what a lot of people in southeast Wisconsin think.

Actually, the belief that a man could turn himself into a wolf was pondered as early as the 16th century in Europe. Although it is argued today that a healthy wolf will very rarely kill a human being, 500 years ago the wolf was feared as a vicious predator who had acquired a strong taste for the meat of homo sapiens. Individuals suspected of turning themselves into were-wolves (old Saxon word *for* "*man*" plus "*wolf*") were tortured or put to death.

The French had their *loup garou* and Haitian sorcerers had *bokors*. Northern European warriors attacked their enemies clad in animal (usually wolf) skins. American Indians living in the Upper Midwest referred to a fierce dog/hyena type of animal as *shunka warak'in* (carrying off dogs). Some Navajo in the Southwestern states still believe in the

---

[1] Verse from *The Wolf Man*, 1941 Universal Pictures

skinwalker. Also, people in Mexico relate stories of a werewolf called *nahual.*

In Greek mythology the God Zeus disguised himself as a human traveler and sought lodging in bad King Lycaon's court. The King recognized Zeus and as retribution decided to feed him a meal of human flesh. Recognizing the abhorrent deception, Zeus lashed out in rage, demolishing the palace and turning Lycaon the *man* (anthropos) into a *wolf* (lykos). Thus was born the word *lycanthropy.* There are two definitions: 1) the magical power to change one's self or another person into a wolf or 2) a mental illness whereby a person imagines that he or she is a wolf and seeks to act the part.

Illustration developed from exhibit at the
International Wolf Center in Ely, MN.

The Christian church condemned lycanthropy as a symbol of evil. Mentally ill persons, believing that they were werewolves under the direction of Satan himself, sometimes killed animals—and occasionally humans.

Movies and TV thrillers from silent films in 1913 such as *The Werewolf,* to more current films such as *Twilight* and *New Moon,* that use elaborate special effects and convincing makeup, promote evil doings of the werewolf. Often scenes showed an involuntary transformation of man into werewolf triggered by a full moon. Most lycanthropic beliefs, however, do not tie the moon to this tradition.

Wisconsin has had many werewolf sightings, mostly in Racine County. Back in 1936, a man spotted a fierce looking hairy wolf-man that stood upright on its hind legs and had features resembling something between an ape and a dog. Supposedly, the creature was digging up an old tribal effigy mound just off a back road near Jefferson, Wisconsin. The man returned to the same place the next evening to find the creature there again. This time it spoke in terrifying throaty tones, muttering something that sounded like "gadara."

Another sighting occurred in 1964 in the same general area. A creature described as seven or eight feet tall and weighing about 400 lbs. scurried across the highway, vaulted over a barbed wire fence, and disappeared into a cornfield. This man also returned to the same spot the next day. Bent and broken corn stalks where he had seen the beast enter the field confirmed any suspicions he might have had regarding the sighting!

In 1972, a woman in Jefferson County said that a "large, unknown animal" matching the same description tried to get into their house. Then the monster mauled a horse in their barn and, a few weeks later, attacked another farm animal.

Most werewolf sightings occurred in the early 1990s. All were in the same general area, but more concentrated in the vicinity of Delevan/Elkhorn. To be specific: Bray Road!

Bray Road intersection near Elkhorn, WI.

The first sighting occurred in the fall of 1989 when farmer Scott Bray (spotted a wolf-like animal in his pasture. Worried about his cattle, he trailed the animal for a while until he lost sight of it.

A short time later, Russell Gest heard rustling in some undergrowth. Peering into the brush, he saw a wolf-like creature standing on two legs in a small clearing. It took a couple of steps towards Gest; he wasted no time in departing the area.

Skip a decade; that's when the sightings really increased!

It was a cool autumn night in 1999. As Lori Endrizzi (fictitious name used in other accounts of her experiences) drove around a curve on Bray Road, she thought she saw a person in a crouched position on the shoulder ahead of her. Slowing

4

down, she approached the person and then passed him, or...it! She later described the beast as having gray-brown hair with a wolf face, fangs and pointed ears. Large muscular arms extended out from its broad hairy chest, much like a human's, but somehow different. The creature had fingers with long claws on their ends. Its eyes were a glowing eerie yellow color: like wolf eyes.

Lori was a bar manager. If she would tell her customers about what she had seen, would they think that she had been tipping a few on the other side of the bar??! Sometime later, Lori came across a picture of a werewolf in a library book. At that point in time she was certain that a werewolf is what she had seen that night while driving down Bray Road.

There were other sightings previous to Lori's, but most were kept quiet for obvious reasons, sometimes mentioned only to a best friend or family member who pledged secrecy.

A dairy farmer saw a strange creature in his pasture. It vanished as he approached it, but left behind huge footprints. Later his wife would get a first-hand look at something that seemed to fit the description of what her husband had seen earlier. As she returned home from work one night about 10:30 p.m., the creature crossed the road in front of her car. It turned to stare at her before ambling on.

A second farmer in the vicinity spotted the strange animal early one morning crouching alongside the road gnawing on something, with its claws out in front of his body much like a raccoon would clutch a piece of road kill.

Another man heard rustling in an area overgrown with weeds. Suddenly a creature appeared, taking a couple of steps forward on its hind legs. The man turned and ran as fast as his legs would carry him, only looking back once. By that time the creature was ambling on all fours and did not seem to be chasing him.

In December 1990 an 11-year old girl and her friend were sledding about a mile and a half from the Bray/Hospital Road intersection. They also saw what they first believed to be a dog. One of the girls called to it, "Here boy." The creature stood on its back legs, took a few awkward steps toward them, dropped back on all fours and started running toward them. As the frightened girls ran home, the creature turned and headed in the opposite direction.

All of these sightings occurred within a 6-mile radius of the above-mentioned intersection (and most of them *very* near to that crossroads). Whether out of fear of ridicule or disbelief—or doubt of what they really saw—nobody really came forward with information about the "Bray Road Beast."

All of that changed very shortly after Lori discovered the picture in a library book and began telling people about her experience. About the same time, eighteen-year-old Doris Gibson (also a fictitious name) had her own werewolf experience.

It was a foggy night, October 31, 1999 when Doris drove near *the* intersection. She thought she hit something on her vehicle's front side. She pulled onto the shoulder about 50 feet from where she felt the "thud," left the engine running and stepped out of the car. She walked to the back of the car to see if she had hit an animal. Then this "dark, hairy form" sprung out of the darkness, running toward her. Doris literally flew back into her car just as the beast jumped onto the trunk. As the car bolted forward, the "thing" slid off the car's damp surface. After returning home, Doris noticed scratches resembling claw marks on the back of her car.

Doris thought it could have been a bear. That same evening she had to pick up her mother's boyfriend's daughter who had been out trick-or-treating with friends. Coming back on Bray Road, she again spotted the creature hunched on the side of the road eating something. This time Doris knew it was *not* a bear!

As she talked excitedly and apprehensively about her encounters the next day, the whole community began to buzz. Persons who previously had related their unusual experiences only to close friends and family members began to come forward to share their tales.

After Lori Endrizzi heard Doris' account, she contacted the local newspaper and the animal shelter to encourage others who had seen the creature to come forward and do the same.

Suddenly there was a stream of wild stories from people who believed they might have information regarding the sightings. Rumors persisted of stolen chickens, missing dogs and cats, and men posing as humane officers attempting to snatch up stray canines. Mutilated animals, most with their throats cut (and one with its heart removed) were allegedly found near an old abandoned house in a wooded area back off Willow Road. There were indications of satanic activity such as occult graffiti and candle wax clinging to grave markers in the local cemetery.

Bray Road needs a "Werewolf Crossing" sign!

Stories slowly died out, but there are still many unanswered questions about the strange happenings during the 1990s in the otherwise pastoral countryside just west of Racine and Kenosha.

Descriptions of sightings prior to 1989 seemed to look more like a sasquatch, or perhaps a cross between Bigfoot and a werewolf. Later descriptions pretty much pinpointed werewolf characteristics.

It has been mentioned that many of the sightings were reported by people who were friends. More than one was a school bus driver. Many sightings were on or close to Halloween. Might it all have been a hoax, fed by friends feigning frenzy? Maybe...but then again....

CHAPTER 2

WHO'S APPEARING AT THE BIOGRAPH?

**Stranger, stop and wish me well,
Just say a prayer for my soul in hell.
I was a good fellow, most people said,
Betrayed by a woman all dressed in red.**[2]

The threesome watched the film *Manhattan Melodrama,* starring Clark Gable, William Powell and Myrna Loy. After the movie the man, accompanied by two women, exited the Biograph Theater on North Lincoln Avenue near downtown Chicago. The head of the Chicago Department of Justice, Mel Purvis, and other law enforcement officers were waiting outside the theatre entrance. Purvis ordered the man to "Halt." The man drew his pistol and kept running. Several shots were fired; the fatal one occurred as the fugitive turned to enter a nearby alleyway.

They finally got him: John Dillinger, famed gangster named Public Enemy No. 1 by J. Edgar Hoover, head of the Federal Bureau of Investigation (FBI). Or did they? Is the figure who haunts the alleyway today really John Dillinger?

John Herbert Dillinger was born June 22, 1903 in Indianapolis. His father was a grocer, a church-going man with high moral standards. His mother

---

[2] Author unknown. Poem appeared on a building near the Biograph Theatre shortly after the shooting.

died of a stroke when Johnnie was only three. We can only guess the reasons why the boy chose the road of crime that eventually ended violently in the alley next to the theatre.

When he was about 10 years old, defiant Johnnie became the leader of a gang of kids called the *Dirty Dozen*. He constantly was in trouble, did poorly in school and was at odds with his father. Finally, after stealing a car and escaping from the police, Johnnie entered the Navy for what would be a short-lived military career. Just five months later he went AWOL, married a sixteen-year-old girl named Beryl Hovious from Martinsville, Indiana, and moved in with his father on a farm in Mooresville.

Soon Johnnie was arrested for stealing chickens. His father worked out a deal with prosecutors, but things were not working out well between father and son. The young married couple soon moved in with *her* parents. Dillinger had difficulty holding a job and the marriage rapidly disintegrated, ending in a divorce.

Then, one Saturday night, a 21-year-old Dillinger assaulted a grocery store clerk in an armed robbery attempt. He pleaded guilty and was sentenced to 10-20 years in prison. In May 1933, after only eight years and some months, Dillinger was paroled.

Less than four months after his release, Dillinger was captured again after robbing several businesses in an attempt to finance a planned prison escape of a few of his cronies. Three weeks later Dillinger's gang sprang *him* in a daring escape, killing the sheriff. The gang continued their crime spree through the Midwest and eventually into Florida and Arizona. A fire broke out in their Tucson hotel, and the men were recognized and promptly arrested.

On January 28, 1934, Dillinger was jailed at Crown Point, Indiana. Here he bragged that no prison could hold him. A month later, aided by a hand-carved wooden pistol (some say it was soap) covered with black shoe polish, he escaped from jail and headed for Iowa and South Dakota.

After making a few "bank withdrawals" along the way, Dillinger and new girlfriend, Billie Frechette, rented an apartment in St. Paul under the names of Mr. and Mrs. Carl T. Hellman. The apartment manager soon became suspicious and notified the FBI. Agents arrived; Billie slammed the door in their face and hurriedly left through a back door with John and Homer Van Meter. Dillinger suffered a leg wound in the escape, and sought medical attention in Minneapolis.

The FBI engaged in a manhunt throughout the Twin Cities. They staked out the apartment and soon observed a cleaning lady trying to retrieve a briefcase left in the Dillinger apartment. When Eddie Green arrived to pick up the case, they order him to stop. He drew his gun and was killed.

Around the fourth of April, John and Billie headed back to his hometown in Indiana, where they attended a family picnic and even posed for some pictures that later would appear frequently in articles about the infamous lawbreaker.

After a short visit, the two headed back to Chicago. They arranged a meeting at a local tavern to discuss finding a new hideout. Billie entered the tavern first to check out the situation. Inside, waiting FBI agents promptly arrested her. John, who has been sitting in the car waiting for an all-clear signal, soon smelled a rat. He slowly drove around the corner and out of sight. Before leaving town, he phoned his attorney to ask him to represent Billie!

Two weeks later John and his gang, along with a few female companions, headed north to Manitowish Waters, Wisconsin to lay low for a few days at Little Bohemia. It is believed that the resort owner, Emil Wanatka Sr., had met some of the gang members a few years before when Wanatka was a popular Chicago restaurateur. Supposedly Dillinger and Wanatka were friends with another Chicago club owner, Louis Cernocky. Also, Dillinger and Wanatka allegedly retained the same lawyer, Louis Piquett. Some accounts say Piquett furnished the wooden gun connected with the Crown Point jailbreak <u>and</u> arranged for the gang to stay at Little Bohemia. Others say Cernocky wrote a letter to Wanatka telling him that he was sending friends up north and asking Wanatka to "treat them well." Still others claim that gang members hung out in Wanatka's Chicago restaurant where he became friends with many from the Chicago underworld.

Regardless of how the gang found out about Little Bohemia, they arrived at the resort the afternoon of Friday, April 20, 1934. They arrived at different times of the day in three automobiles. There was John Dillinger, John Hamilton and his girlfriend Pat Cherington, Homer Van Meter and his girlfriend Marie Comforti, as well as Baby-Face Nelson (Lester Gillis) and his wife Helen, Tommy Carroll and his wife Jean. Pat Reilly, a friend of the gang, was there too. The group paid handsomely for their somewhat abbreviated retreat.

Little Bohemia Lodge in Manitowish Waters, Wisconsin.

All appeared well, but there was some uneasiness it seemed. Baby-Face Nelson played catch with the Wanatka's 8-year-old son, Emil Jr. He threw the ball so hard that he made young Wanatka cry.

The Wanatkas were being carefully watched and their phone calls monitored. Nan Wanatka received permission to take Emil Jr. to a family birthday party at the home of her brother. Suspicious by nature, the meanest of the crew, Baby-Face, followed Nan. Nan noticed and was able to elude Nelson. She gave her brother a letter written by Emil to be mailed to the Attorney General's office in Chicago. At the party Nan quietly got word out about the guests at Little Bohemia. Sensing the urgency of the matter, she and her brother-in-law, Henry Voss, developed a new plan. Voss would stop by Little Bohemia and bum a pack of cigarettes off of Nan. If Emil agreed to Voss contacting the Feds by phone, there would be a note hidden in the pack. Voss would then drive to Rhinelander to make the phone call alerting Mel Purvis to the current situation.

Feds arrived in Rhinelander the afternoon of Sunday, April 22, to be informed through Henry's wife (Nan's sister) that the gang had changed their plans and would be leaving the resort earlier than planned. They hastily put together a plan and drove to Manitowish Waters that snowy April evening under the cover of darkness. With such short notice, cars had to be obtained for the trip. Two of them broke down along the way, and some of the agents had to ride on the running boards for the remainder of the trip.

As they arrived at Little Bo, the Wanatka's dogs started to bark. Three local men, coincidentally just leaving the restaurant, were assumed to be gang members. They quickly got into their car and proceeded to drive down the long entrance road. Feds shouted for them to stop, but with their car radio blaring and the dogs barking, they didn't hear the commands. The Feds fired at the men, killing one instantly and wounding the other two.

Alerted by the gunfire, Dillinger and a couple of other men ran upstairs to retrieve their money and guns. Firing back at the law enforcement officials, they escaped through the windows of their second-story rooms. Others broke out bar windows and fled from the side of the building. An embankment along the water shielded the men from view. Dillinger, along with Van Meter and Hamilton, ran west along the lake. They stole a vehicle from a guest at a nearby lodge and drove on a less traveled county road toward Minneapolis.

Baby-Face Nelson ran the other way. Nelson came to a nearby home where he forced the residents to drive him south on Highway 51. They had car trouble and drove into Koerner's Resort with their lights off. The Koerners had been alerted to the activities at Little Bohemia and promptly called to report the suspicious car. Agents showed up in a few minutes. Nelson walked calmly to their auto and riddled the agents with machine gun fire. They all escaped the car, but Carter Baum died trying to escape over a fence about 40 feet away. Constable Christensen collapsed and Agent Newman escaped into the woods and was able to make it to a nearby resort. A local newspaper described the bungled raid on Little Bohemia as "one of the biggest fiascoes in the annals of criminal history."

Pat Cherrington and Pat Reilly had gone to St. Paul—some say to collect a large sum of money owed them. They were just returning to the lodge when they noticed the federal agents at the gate. They quickly turned out the headlights of the car and shifted the car into reverse. The FBI shot out a tire in the car, but the two managed to escape the scene, stop in Mercer to change the tire, and head back to the Twin Cities.

Meanwhile, the Dillinger faction found its way to Minnesota too. Here police identified the car and gave pursuit. Hamilton was badly injured by bullets fired into the car. The gang ditched their pursuers, stole another car and headed for Aurora, Illinois where Hamilton died. Dillinger and Van Meter decided to lay low.

Baby-Face Nelson had car troubles and ended up walking for miles to Lac du Flambeau where he holed up for a few days with a Native American named Ollie Catfish before stealing another car and heading back to Chicago. (Nelson was killed by agents on November 27, 1934 in a gunfight near

Barrington. One story says that his naked body was dumped about 20 miles from the shooting, supposedly to slow identification.)

Sometime during the following weeks Dillinger had plastic surgery removing some moles, a scar from his face and the cleft from his chin. Work was done on his nose as well.

That summer John found a new girlfriend, Polly Hamilton. They attended ball games and movies, went out to dinner—pretty much a normal lifestyle. Although she was teased for dating a man that looked a lot like John Dillinger, Polly supposedly thought that her new beau was Jimmy Lawrence, a clerk and small-time lawbreaker who had moved to Chicago from Wisconsin. He bore an uncanny resemblance to John, and he lived in a nearby neighborhood.

Polly was renting a room from Anna Sage who lived with her son on Chicago's north side. Anna, a brothel owner, was facing deportation to her home country, Romania. When she was certain she had determined that the man Polly was dating was actually John Dillinger, she contacted a policeman she knew. Secret meetings were held, and Melvin Purvis was brought into the talks. Purvis, along with Sam Cowley, who replaced him after the Little Bohemia debacle, made a deal with Anna. They would do everything within their power to prevent her deportation, and give her a nice reward as well, if she would cooperate in a plan to capture Dillinger.

On Sunday, July 22, 1934, Anna called authorities with information that she and Polly would be going to a movie with John that night at either the Marbro or the Biograph Theater. She would wear a dark orange skirt for identification purposes. Agents staked out both places. When it became known that the three had gone to the Biograph, they immediately congregated outside that theater. A couple of the agents actually walked up and down the aisles periodically (amazingly without being observed) to make sure that Dillinger was still inside.

It was easy to spot the small group exiting the theater after the movie. They were among the first out of the building. Pistols drawn, Purvis yelled to Dillinger, "Halt!" Dillinger immediately drew his Colt automatic and ran for the alley. Three bullets brought him down at the alley entrance. Purvis spoke to the fallen man; there was no answer.

An autopsy was performed on the dead man. Reports say that he had brown eyes and a heart condition. Dillinger had blue/grey eyes. His service records, though recorded when John was years younger, showed his heart to be in perfect condition. Some viewers did not recognize the body. Even Dillinger's father purportedly exclaimed, "That's not my son." The man who was killed was said to be heavier and shorter than Dillinger (though other accounts vary only by an inch or two and five or ten lbs.) While Dillinger had undergone plastic surgery, he still had some scars remaining on his body— missing on the corpse. Some believed it was Jimmy Lawrence, the look-alike small-time hood Polly Hamilton thought she was dating!

If Anna figured out that Polly's boyfriend was posing as Lawrence, could she have told Polly? Was Polly in on a plan to bait the real Jimmy Lawrence to take them to the movie that night? Maybe John was in on it as well. Lawrence supposedly was never seen again after that fateful night. Might it even be possible that a humiliated FBI agency covered up what the girls set up? Will the entire truth ever be known?

Mannequin at entrance to the Biograph Theatre
portrays Polly Hamilton as the "Lady in Red."

Below the mannequin in the window is a plaque that reads:

Chicago Landmark

Biograph Theater
Samuel N. Crowen, architect
1914

Perhaps best known for its historical connection to the infamous gangster John Dillinger, this building is also one of Chicago's oldest remaining neighborhood movie theaters. Its design typifies the first-generation movie houses whose architectural style gave legitimacy and respectability to the fledgling motion picture industry. Dillinger's death here in 1934, after being named "Public Enemy No.1" by the F.B.I., also guarantees the Biograph's place in Chicago crime history.

Designated on March 28, 2001
Richard M. Daley, Mayor
Commission on Chicago Landmarks

Anna Sage was deported to Romania where she died in 1947. Purvis supposedly was so distressed by the fact that Hoover reneged on the deal with Anna that he committed suicide in 1960.

There were reports of persons receiving letters from Dillinger in the years following his death, originating from somewhere on the west coast, probably Oregon. Nagging questions were left unanswered.

Note: I live in Manitowish Waters, a few miles from Little Bo. Numerous newspaper articles of these notorious gangsters adorn the lobby. Bullet holes in the windows and walls have been preserved. Memorabilia and paraphernalia left behind that night in April 1934 are exhibited in one of the rooms. Also on display is a chair from the Biograph Theater in Chicago. (It could even be *the* seat from which Dillinger watched his last movie!)

My next-door neighbor, Larry Nerby, passed away recently at age 96. He had related a story to me years ago regarding the development of a friendship with a former Gary, Indiana police chief, Walter Conroy, who came to northern Wisconsin to hunt deer. The law enforcement officer had been involved in the manhunt for Dillinger and was a participant in the shooting at the Biograph. Conroy offered to buy a snowmobile for Larry's children. As promised, cash was sent on a weekly basis until the snowmobile was paid for. The police chief was very elusive when asked why he suddenly seemed to have a lot of money, but had previously told Larry that he had been the closest one to John Dillinger when he was gunned down in Chicago. Did Conroy kill Dillinger and if so, was it reward money? Payoff from other mob-related activities? Or (remember Jimmy Lawrence?) was it something else? Or maybe nothing else.

The reproduction newspaper, *Historical FishWrap*, states that, in addition to the federal officers, four police officers from Chicago and Indiana were involved in the stakeout at the Biograph that night. Federal agents could not accept a reward for killing John Dillinger, but police officers were told they could. The glory was left for the feds. This seems to substantiate the story told by my neighbor.

Magazine suggests reward money was paid to police officers.

Who is the ghost that sometimes is seen running down the alleyway near 2433 Lincoln Avenue in Chicago? Bob and I walked down that alley and behind the Biograph Theater. Although it was a cool day in April, we did not feel the icy chills that other mystery seekers had noticed, nor did we have feelings of uneasiness in that alleyway—at least not related to ghosts!

We stopped in a Mexican restaurant next door to the Biograph, ordered a beverage, and asked our waiter a few questions. He was a young college student from somewhere in central Mexico. He knew casi nada, not even what time the Biograph opened. Although the sign in the window advertised the next movie would be showing at 3 p.m., the theatre was not yet open at 4 p.m. It seemed that it had been closed for business. *Wikipedia* reports that live productions are shown now at the theater.

Life pretty much goes on as usual here. Almost everyone has heard of John Dillinger, but he is thought of infrequently.

Biograph Theater is on the left side of the picture.

Today the "El" passes over Lincoln Street.

In the spring of 2006 moviemakers arrived in Wisconsin to film the movie, *Public Enemies*, depicting the Dillinger's life. Filming began in Columbus, Wisconsin—a perfect setting with its older buildings reminiscent of the time period when the Dillinger gang terrorized the Midwest. Here the Greencastle, Indiana bank robbery scene was filmed.

Next, the film team moved Oshkosh: Here they shot scenes of the arrival of federal agents with captive Dillinger via a 1929 Ford Tri-motor plane borrowed from the Oshkosh Experimental Aircraft Assn. depicting the transfer of prisoner Dillinger from Arizona to Chicago; a Sioux Falls bank robbery filmed in a reconstructed block of downtown Oshkosh and scenes shot in the New Moon Café (known as the Skalsa Restaurant in the movie).

Extras wait outside near the Blue Moon Café in Oshkosh.

Then the film crew moved on to Manitowish Waters where Dillinger and his gang had their famous shoot-out with federal and state agents. The area received its claim to fame once again as Johnny Depp (playing John Dillinger) and fellow actors relived the famous shootout on the 74th anniversary of the event. Other scenes for the movie were filmed in Milwaukee, Madison, Beaver Dam, Wisconsin Dells, and Darlington, Wisconsin as well as locations in Indiana and Illinois.

Public Enemies costars Christian Bale as Melvin Purvis and Marion Cotillard as Billie Frechette. The movie is based on a book authored by Bryan Burrough of the same title. Director Michael Mann was born in Chicago and became interested in film making while attending the University of Wisconsin in the mid 1960s. He is known for his attention to authenticity and detail.

Did John die in front of the Biograph Theatre in Chicago that night? Or, did he live out his life somewhere in Oregon and/or other western locations under an assumed name? Does his spirit linger on Lincoln Street, still hiding from those who attempted to determine his fate? Or is the wispy figure sometimes spotted running into the alley way really the ghost of look-alike hood, Jimmy Lawrence? Interested people want to know.

CHAPTER 3

MARY STILL TARRIES

**"And as the evening darkens, lo! How bright,
Through the deep purple of the twilight air,
Beams forth the radiance of its light,
With strange, unearthly splendor in the glare!**[3]

The radiant light that night, March 6, 1886 did not emanate from the fourth order Fresnel lens atop the 41-foot tall brick tower attached to the Sand Point Lighthouse, but from the blaze-orange flames that shot high into the dark sky. The building was almost completely destroyed, but an urgent question bothered fire fighters: Where was the lighthouse keeper, Mary Terry?

We go back to the year 1864. Escanaba was a growing community on a natural harbor of Lake Michigan's Little Bay De Noc. The Peninsula Railroad was extended into Escanaba from nearby iron mines at Negaunee, about 45 miles to the northwest as the seagull flies! At the docks on the Bay, the iron would be loaded onto ore boats heading for steel mills located in Indiana, Ohio and Illinois.

With increased traffic into and out of the harbor, not only from the mines but also from the fishing and lumber industries, it soon became evident that a navigational aid was badly needed here. So, in 1867

---

[3] From *The Lighthouse*, Henry Wadsworth Longfellow

funds were appropriated by the National Lighthouse Service to build the Sand Point Lighthouse. It was a two-toned brown brick building, with an attached brick tower topped by a cast iron lantern room. The fixed red light warned ships of the sand reef that extended out into the bay. The light first cast out over the bay on May 13, 1868.

John Terry was appointed to be the first keeper of the lighthouse, but he died of consumption (a disease similar to tuberculosis) before the structure was completed. Escanaba citizens knew John's wife to be a very competent, cool-headed, and methodical woman. They campaigned that she should be commissioned to replace her husband. So, despite some reluctance from the government officials, Mary Terry was assigned as the Keeper at Sand Point. For eighteen years she prevailed at that location. But, it was well known around the area that Mary lived alone in this lighthouse in a remote, quiet area on the outskirts of Escanaba. Many thought that she was a woman of means who may have stashed some of her money somewhere inside the Sand Point lighthouse.

Sometime before 1 a.m. on a cold night in March 1886, a fire broke out in the lighthouse. Deep snow hindered fire fighters from reaching the building in time to save it. After the flames were quenched and the coals had cooled, they entered what was left of the lighthouse. All that remained was the spiral staircase in the tower. The men quickly made their way to what was Mary's bedroom on the north side of the (former) living quarters, but found nothing. They stumbled through the rubble into the oil room on the southeast side of the building. A fireman spotted a soot-covered figure lying on the floor. "Oh, my God...." Investigators found a door still partially standing. It appeared that it had been forced open as the bolt had been pushed forward.

Many townsfolk found it difficult to believe that this was an accident because of Mary's thoroughness, attention to detail, and overall competence. But there were other nagging questions in their mind. Did she encounter an intruder in the oil room? Was she trying to extinguish the blaze herself? Was the blaze a cover-up for a murder? Was a handyman's description of his conversation with Mary the day before the fire accurate? The man related that he told Mary the firewood beside the stove was hot and could be dangerous. He mentioned that Mary replied that it was a concern, but said "she slept with one eye open." Was it a little too coincidental that the blaze occurred the very next day after that conversation? Was the handyman, or possibly another intruder, trying to cover up a robbery gone bad?

A six-man jury was appointed to investigate the cause of Mary's death. Although there wasn't much evidence left in the badly charred lighthouse to examine, a few gold pieces belonging to Mary were found lying on the floor, and pieces of important papers, burnt around the edges, informed the finders that, if she should die, Mary's savings of approximately $4,000 would be divided amongst her nieces and nephew.

After the fire, the Coast Guard rebuilt the structure and returned the light to service. In 1935 a harbor light was installed a quarter mile offshore, making the Sand Point light obsolete. This light is still in use today. It marks the sunken wreckage of what is left of the steamer Nahant. The ore ship burned at a dock here on November 9, 1997.

Harbor Light.

The U.S. Coast Guard took over responsibility from the National Lighthouse Service for all navigational lights in 1939. At that time the Sand Point lens was removed, tower lowered, and roof raised to create a second story that later provided housing for Coast Guard personnel.

The County Historical Society negotiated a long-term lease with the Coast Guard and obtained funding, They retrieved the original blueprints from the archives, and over the next several years restored the lighthouse to its 1867 status. The roof was raised to its pre-1939 level. Windows, once installed by the Coast Guard, were removed. The Society was able to replicate the former lantern by obtaining one from another abandoned lighthouse. The Fresnel lens was pulled out of storage in Menominee.

Restored Sand Point Lighthouse in
Escanaba's Ludington Park.

We walked up the cement sidewalk, noting that the light tower faced us, not the lake, in front of the building. The red brick building, painted white, is set back from the peninsula point. In fact, it is located on the very beginning of the peninsula that is connected to the mainland.

We stopped for a moment to gaze at a plywood statue of former Keeper Mary Terry; then we entered the museum.

Mary Terry stands outside the entrance
of Sand Point Lighthouse.

The restored museum is decorated with authentic
19th-century furnishings. One room contains old
newspaper articles, pictures and memorabilia from
that time period. Artifacts from the Nahant can be
found here too.

Just inside, we were greeted by a congenial Delta
County Historical Society volunteer, Betty Lundin.
We asked Betty about the rumored ghost of Mary
Terry that allegedly inhabits the building. Betty
affirmed the allegation, smiling. She then added,
"Mary Terry doesn't bother me because I clean her
house every spring!"

Tour guide Betty Lundin.

Betty related a conversation that she had with another volunteer at the lighthouse. The woman found a hat lying on the floor of the upstairs bedroom when she came into work one morning. That hat had been secured firmly onto the head of a mannequin the night before.

Others have heard doors in the building slam shut when nobody was there. One museum attendant believes that the ghost of Mary Terry walks across Little Bay de Noc and sometimes wanders through the walls of the lighthouse, just checking to make sure everything is still in order.

But everything is not in order; something is wrong. As when it was first constructed, the tower still faces Escanaba, not Lake Michigan. Something is also very wrong about the circumstances of the fire that night in March 1886. It seems the truth may never be known regarding the blaze that destroyed the original Sand Point Lighthouse and concealed the cause of the death of Keeper Mary Terry.

Mary knows, and her spirit remains at the place where she kept the light for so many years. If her death was a murder, one could believe that her perpetrator is in perpetuity experiencing an inferno of his own.

CHAPTER 4

GULLIVER'S GHOULS AND BUOYS

"The rocky ledge runs far into the sea,
And on its outer point, some miles away,
The lighthouse lifts its massive masonry,
A pillar of fire by night, of cloud by day."[4]

Seul Choix—Harbor of Refuge.
(A ghostly white form seems to appear on the sign's right side.)

Jim Barr has a connection to the old lighthouse at Seul Choix (pronounced *Sis Shwa*) Point located near Gulliver, Michigan--about 15 miles east of Manistique. Jim married a lighthouse keeper's

---

[4] From *The Lighthouse*, Henry Wadsworth Longfellow.

daughter: the late Shirley Blanchard Barr. Shirley's dad, Bill Blanchard, assumed the keeper position at Seul Choix on August 10, 1910. He was promoted from first assistant after the former keeper, Captain Joseph "Willy" Townshend, passed away.

Barr, a member of the Gulliver Historical Society and a volunteer tour guide at Seul Choix, greets my friend, Gerry, and me as we enter the impressive well-maintained lighthouse. He is about to start his introductory spiel. I explain that I am a writer of ghost stories and would like information to use in a story about the lighthouse and its ghost. He is more than happy to accommodate my request. I ask if I may take pictures for use in this book, and he graciously agrees to pose for a photo.

My (film) camera does not seem to be working properly. I check the battery level; it seems to be okay. The camera was working fine just a few minutes ago when I snapped a few shots around the grounds outside of the lighthouse. Barr dismisses the malfunction. "A lot of people have problems with their cameras in here." It seems as though the psychic atmosphere within the building can raise havoc with batteries. While I am getting more and more frustrated, Gerry shoots off a picture with her digital camera. I don't understand; her camera operates with a battery too!

Barr begins the tour with a little bit of history of the area. He relates how mid 18th century French fur traders, headed for the Straits of Mackinac (about 60 miles west) in their voyageur canoes, came ashore at this spot. When storms whipped up the great Lake Michigan, they took refuge in the only safe, or protected, harbor in the area. In the French language, Seul Choix translates to "only choice" in English.

Jim Barr, volunteer tour guide at Seul Choix.

By the early 1800s a thriving fishing village existed along the harbor's shore. About 300 settlers and an equal number of American Indians lived here peacefully. They worked together, supporting their families through fishing or working for the lighthouse service.

There was a one-room schoolhouse in the community. One of the keeper's duties was to hire the school marm to teach kindergarten through eighth grade. She would be paid an annual salary of $423. Her duties were varied: keep the fire going, do light maintenance and, of course, instill knowledge to a varied age group with different interests and skill levels.

Logging companies and stone quarries sprang up in the area, and shipping commerce increased proportionately. There were some dangerous shoals near Seul Choix Point and no lights to guide the vessels. So Congress appropriated the necessary funds, and a lighthouse and fog signal were completed in 1895.

The land slopes down to where a limestone shoal
extends 100 yards out in the water.

Barr presented a fascinating background of Seul Choix Point; but I needed to know: "Why is the lighthouse here referred to as "the most haunted lighthouse on the Great Lakes?"

Barr continued his story. Captain Townshend was born in Bristol, England in 1847. Diagnosed with tuberculosis at age 18, his doctor suggested he try saltwater sailing for a cure. So Townshend became a captain of a small schooner, but in time met a woman he wanted to marry. She persuaded him to live on dry land! Eventually they moved to the

United States, and Townshend signed on with the Lighthouse Service. In 1901 he came to Seul Choix. Townshend served as Light Keeper here until cancer claimed his life. Near the end, in pain and agony, his screams reportedly could be heard at a nearby boarding house. He died in August 1910 in his upstairs bedroom. His body was embalmed in the basement and then held in the parlor of the lighthouse until relatives could arrive to pay their last respects.

Shadows creep onto and into the Seul Choix Lighthouse.
The replica birdhouse was built from a fish box by former
Light Keeper, Willard Hanson.

After Townshend's death other keepers came and went until 1973 when the light was automated. Over the next decade the abandoned property fell into disrepair. In June 1977 the Michigan Department of Natural Resources purchased the property from the Coast Guard, and in October 1987 the Gulliver

Historical Society was formed with the purpose of funding and restoring the buildings. It was during this restoration period that workers began to sense a supernatural presence.

According to Barr, a carpenter was working alone in the locked building one day. As he was chiseling out tile on the ground floor, he thought that he heard someone walking upstairs. When he stopped his work, the steps would stop. He called out, "Who's there?" There was no response. This happened twice. The third time he put down his hammer to listen. "He could tell someone was on the top of the stairs and was on the way down," Barr remembers. The carpenter left hurriedly and never returned to work in the building again!

In April 2004, before the tourist season, Barr himself was doing some plastering at the lighthouse. He heard a knock at the main door, and hollered, "Come on in." When nobody entered, he came down the ladder and opened the door. Nobody was there. No cars were in the parking lot, and there were no footprints in the snow. The next time he heard a knock, Jim addressed the suspected culprit, "Leave me alone Captain Townshend; I have work to do." The knocking stopped.

Townshend liked to smoke cigars, but his wife forbade him to smoke in the house. Now his spirit seems to be getting even—the smell of cigars comes and goes; tour guides and visitors alike frequently get a whiff of the offensive odor. Then, within a few seconds, the stench is gone.

In 1997 a three-person media team from Saginaw spent the night at Seul Choix to do a documentary on the the restoration there. Fredrick Stonehouse, in his book *Haunted Lakes II*, tells of experiences that turned their attention from restoration to exploration of ghostly activities! The crew, along with a clairvoyant and his wife, spent the night at the lighthouse in sleeping bags near the parlor.

Sheet music on top of the piano changed positions three times; so did the silverware on the dining room table. The crew saw two face-like images in the upstairs bedroom mirror (one turned into a skull before it disappeared; the other strongly resembled Captain Townshend). A cameraman saw a shadowy figure cross the hall near the parlor, and another became physically ill after a strong odor overcame him. A video camera failed to record visuals but left an unexplained "whooshing" sound.

The media team also did an experiment with cigars, placing two stogies upstairs and two downstairs in different locations throughout the building. When they crawled out of their sleeping bags the next morning, the two "downstairs" cigars were missing— found later in the pocket of a mannequin's uniform. The hat on the dummy had been turned around backwards! The cigars that were left upstairs seemed to be undisturbed.

In 1999 two Eagle Scouts, doing research on ghosts, spent the night in the lighthouse with their Scoutmaster: our guide Jim Barr! They put a new twist on the above-mentioned experiment, using three differently priced cigars.

Later that night they discovered one of the cheaper cigars had been moved from the third banister on the stairs down to the second banister. About 3:30 a.m. they awoke to a noise and noticed the other inexpensive cigar placed in the dining room had been moved to the kitchen. The expensive cigar remained in its original placement!

Barr described to us another incident he experienced earlier that night. "About 10 p.m. I was looking into the dining room when I saw a bird going across the top of the windows, fluttering, flying, moving—but more of a shadow." Then it suddenly disappeared.

The Boy Scouts heard recurring noises upstairs and occasionally smelled obnoxious odors. And they too had problems with camera battery malfunction.

Several years ago several pieces of an oak table belonging to Townshend were found in the basement. The table was reconstructed and placed in the kitchen. Today, the table is set in the tradition style of our country: fork on the left of the plate, knife and spoon on the right. Remember, Townshend was raised in England. The British way of placing silverware in a place setting differed from ours. Often staff members arriving at the lighthouse in the morning will find the fork above the plate, tines turned downward. Townsend just likes to be correct!

Captain Townshend rearranges silverware.
(Museum photo)

Townshend has been seen on the grounds briefly; then vanishes into thin air with the blink of an eye.

Visitors have caught a glimpse of the Captain looking out of an upstairs window. Others have seen his face emerge from a haze on the upstairs mirror.

There is an old superstition that a mirror must be completely covered when there is a death in the house or the victim's spirit might move into it. If Townshend's spirit did not move in to the mirror, it sometimes goes there for a visit!

Writer Jan Langley spent some time at the lighthouse with Marilyn Fischer, president of the Gulliver Historical Society. During one visit, as the two were conversing in the lighthouse kitchen, Marilyn suddenly became quiet. Langley describes the occurrence. "Beads of perspiration formed on her forehead...Marilyn started to shake all over. I reached for her and grabbed her hand. A frigid wall of air circled us. My spine was ice and chills covered my hands and legs."

Suddenly everything returned to normal. Jan questioned Marilyn, "What happened to you"

"I could see him, Jan. Over there by the back door. He just stood there and watched us."

At that point Jan looked out the kitchen window at a darkened lamp and spontaneously addressed the spirit. "If that was you, Captain Townshend, blink twice." The light blinked once, then again!

A video of the ghostly activities here can be seen in the building that houses the gift shop. There is a separate viewing room with seating for several people. Ask for the video with the amazing mirror scene! It has not been enhanced or doctored. This 1998 video received the prestigious Telly Award; the plaque hangs on the wall here.

Life goes on at the lighthouse. Chairs slide across the floor, mirrors fog up and develop images, doors open and close, cameras don't work, the heavy open Bible on the stand slams shut, voices and footsteps emanate from the tower and fingerprints appear on the freshly shined lens. Then, there's that terrible cigar smell, often accompanied by isolated cold spots! Jim's wife, Marie, smelled it too. Another time Marie witnessed the refrigerator door open by itself and remarked to Jim, "See he's here again today."

There is more going on down the road from the lighthouse in the Gulliver area. Spirits are said to wander through walls in old houses in the village. There are rumors of sealed rooms and mysterious underground chambers, apparitions in windows, unidentified voices, skeletal remains, and strange unexplainable occurrences. An area hunter, James Goudreau, and his cocker spaniel, Spot, walked by the house where his grandmother used to live. He saw a pretty woman in the upstairs window of the vacant house who he believes could be the spirit of his great aunt's niece, though she actually lived next door.

A local resident saw a young woman in a long white dress come up from the beach and walk down their road. They recognized her from old photographs as a woman who had died half a century earlier.

Goudreau saw an apparition in an upstairs window.

Ghostly black shapes known as "rock spirits" have been seen meandering in small groups along the shoreline under darkening skies. A previous home owner who lived on this street claimed he often saw the black figures moving down his hallway and passing through the walls—perhaps continuing along the old trail that the foundation of the house now rests upon. Though these spirits were not considered evil, priests were sometimes called in. If you see rosaries or crosses hung in trees, it is probably where the mystical figures were seen.

Watching for rock spirits.

Maudie Lockhart, a volunteer at Seul Choix, tells of her experience at the historic Old Deerfield Resort on the sandy shores of nearby Gulliver Lake. She had been a cleaning person there. While stripping floors one day, she looked up to see a headless torso wearing a plaid flannel shirt "come in the front door and float through the bedroom door!" She believes the apparition was a man who had constructed cabins at the resort and hung himself when he was in his seventies.

On another occasion, Maudie's son was doing some work inside the building when he heard the shower running in the bathroom. "Mom, go turn the shower off," he shouted from the other room. Maudie walked into the bathroom, but there was no water coming from the shower...and all was quiet.

As mentioned, the Seul Choix lighthouse and the surrounding Gulliver area seem to be haunted by several spirits. One thing that seems to be apparent, however, is that Captain Townshend is the most active spirit for miles around, especially during periods when remodeling is being done at the lighthouse. (This coincidence has been observed at other haunted lighthouses as well.)

Joseph W. Townshend was buried at Lakeview Cemetery in Manistique, Michigan--Section 12, Lot 2, Grave 5 to be exact. But something tells me that the benevolent revenant prefers the haunts at Seul Choix Point!

CHAPTER 5

THE KEY TO ROOM 310

Last thing I remember
I was running for the door
I had to find the passage
Back to the place I was before.
Relax said the nightman
We are programmed to receive.
You can check out any time you like
But you can never leave.[5]

The Historic Karsten Inn in Kewaunee, Wisconsin is a lovely place...such a lovely place.

The key to Room 310 will unlock the door, but it hasn't succeeded in unlocking the mysteries of this room where the third-floor maid, "Agatha," resided from 1925 to 1937.

The same goes for Room 205—where little Billy Karsten spent time with his grandfather, William, owner of the hotel from 1911 to 1928. (The Karstens resided in a suite of rooms—205 through 210.)

Don Hayden stayed in both rooms. His job brought him to town for several weeks in late 2004. He made reservations at the Karsten, right downtown, with a restaurant on the premises...and, they offered him a discounted monthly rate.

---

[5] From *Hotel California*, The Eagles

The Karsten Inn, known as the Steamboat Inn when it was built in 1858, went through a series of names as well as a series of owners. William Karsten bought the hotel in 1911. A fire totally destroyed the wooden structure on Valentine's Day 1912, but it was rebuilt that same year (a three-story, 52-room luxurious brick hotel) and renamed The Hotel Karsten.

William Karsten sold the hotel to his son in 1928. When he died of a heart attack in his suite of rooms in January 1940, William Jr. took over total management of the hotel. In August 1964 William Jr. died, also of a heart attack. The hotel closed for a couple of years and fell into disrepair. The building was scheduled to be razed, when two brothers purchased it. The hotel passed through another series of owners, and in May 2001 the Heuers, purchased it.

Totally renovated to its original splendor of the mid-1890s, The Historic Karsten Inn became a showcase of unusual furniture from the past and an atmosphere from another century. Yet, it has all the amenities and conveniences of today: air conditioning, radio alarm clocks, satellite TV, telephones with voicemail and data ports, hair dryers, and coffee makers. Some rooms even have Jacuzzi tubs.

Hayden checked into Room 310, had a bite to eat, and unpacked his luggage. He treasured his gold jewelry. He had a ritual when he traveled of removing the pieces every night and placing them on top of his closed briefcase lying on its side next to the bed.

Soon Don drifted into a light sleep. His wife rolled over, put her arm around him, and gave him a big hug. Don opened his eyes with a start—"Wait a minute; my wife is in California!" He was alone in bed, but had the uneasy feeling that this was not a dream.

The next morning he awoke to find his briefcase standing upright and the jewelry lying on the side of the table! "I've had it; I'm out of here." The desk clerk assigned him to Room 205.

Edye, a good friend of mine, lives near Casco, just a few miles down the road from Kewaunee. A business associate of Don's, she suggested that we meet at the gift shop where she worked. He would be there, and I could then hear first hand of his experiences.

I arrived in Kewaunee mid-afternoon on a Friday, along with my husband Bob, Edye's daughter Roxanne, and her granddaughters Elise and Emily. Our first stop was the gift shop!

During our conversation, I asked Don why he had checked into not one, but two of the most actively "haunted" rooms in the hotel! Don responded that he didn't know about the reputation of the hotel. Because he was by himself, he was assigned to smaller rooms. Also, visitors at the nearby nuclear power plant had reserved many of the Karsten Inn's 23 sleeping rooms.

He told me about his experiences in Room 310, concluding with, "The hair stood up on the back of my neck."

"Did a switch to Room 205 change anything?"

"Well, the first night in this room little Billy bounced his ball all night long; I scarcely slept."

"Who is little Billy?"

Roxanne and Emily gaze at a portrait of Billy III.

"Did you see the picture of the child in the lobby—it's William Karsten III. Families staying here sometimes find that their young children wander out into the halls to play with a little boy. Later, when they're in the lobby, their youngster will point to the picture and say 'That's him!' Billy is a prankster; he hides things on you."

"Like what?"

"On Saturday I went down to do my laundry. I put the detergent in the washer, sat around for a while, then came back to load the clean clothes into the dryer, and noticed the hand towels were gone. Billy hid them."

"*Ohhh K....!* Anything else?"

Yes. That night, or rather the next morning— it was about 2:00 or 2:30 a.m., I felt the bed move, as if a person sat down at the foot of it.

48

I didn't see anyone, but there was an indentation—like someone was sitting there! And, I kept hearing someone turning my doorknob throughout the night.

The next week I arranged for one of our employees and her husband to tour the Karsten. I stayed in the lobby while the desk clerk took them upstairs.

That couch in the foyer on the third floor? Agatha keeps the pillows a certain way. Before they toured the third floor, they rearranged the pillows. Then they spent a few minutes looking at a few of the rooms. When they came back past the couch, the pillows were back in their original position."

Agatha wouldn't like this arrangement!

Don related a conversation he had at the bar one evening with one of those guys from the nuclear plant who had an experience of his own to share.

I stay here frequently when I come to town. But one night I was pushed down the stairs! I had an argument with my fiancé and left her sitting in the bar to go back up to our room. On the first landing I felt this force give me a shove, and I landed back down in the lobby. Luckily I wasn't seriously hurt. You know Agatha doesn't like men who drink. Supposedly, a drunken farmer raped her when she was only twenty-one. She kept the child, a daughter, and worked here to support her. I hear she was in love with old-man Karsten too.

I had to learn more about Agatha and the Karstens. So we all checked into the Historic Karsten Inn.

I started by reading the journals in our room (310) and the room across the hall (309) where Edye, Roxanne, Elise and Emily were staying.

The latest entry in the book in our room, dated November 6-7, 2004, read:

Tour of the basement from the bartender. Weird smells and a pipe moving on its own. Got a huge orb x 2 on my digital camera. Then in the hallway, the dresser drawer opened, and when I took a picture of the hallway, there was something in the mirror. Lot of bumps in the night and someone whispering "psst." Mirror kept moving.

Entries in the journal from 309 included:

Boy up and down bouncing his ball. The bouncing ball sound happened once outside my door. Then heard a drop of water as though dropping into a pan about 3' from my head. Also got a chill and felt like someone was crawling over me.

Rose/floral scent upstairs hallway near Room 309.

And from Room 210:

> Two ghost hunters are staying on the 3rd floor. They were outside of Room 209. Their machines indicated an entity as they called it. The woman took a digital picture, and it was two orbs of light on each side of the door. It was awesome to see. She said that on her computer these orbs have faces.

> Note: The "ghost hunters" took videos supposedly showing hangers swaying. Tapping noises were heard.

> Felt someone tap my shoulder; my partner was asleep.

> An intense smell of vanilla (by someone who hates vanilla smell).

> Watching Packer games—entertainment doors closed by themselves.

> Creaks and clanks in the night—think this place might be haunted.

And Room 205:

> Noises around 1:00-1:30 a.m. The pen moved around a bit. The ghost messed with me a bunch.

> Video tape sounds like "Aah." Also giggles were heard from Rooms 205-206 and children running. (Note: this comment was from the group mentioned below.)

Three men and three women from "Wisconsin Ghost Investigations" entered notes in the Guest Book that sits on a table in the lobby. They are dated 12/29/01, 7:40 p.m., with observations from different rooms:

205	Hear movement of objects. Enter room. EMF beeps briefly.
207	Hot spot few seconds. Temp. rose 10 degrees on digital thermometer.
208	Heater on and blowing warm air, but room never warms up.
209	Hangers on wall sway in unison. Orb appears over David's head and streams down the side of his body and disappears at legs.
Hall	Running noises.

The next entry is at 8:30 p.m.

Bar	EMF meter beeps on bar stool. Dave felt someone stroke his hair toward the back of his neck. Video and audiotape, sounds of breaking forcefully a few times. Rachel has an EVP (ghost voice) of a male ordering a "Kesslers" in a large whisper—only Rachel, her husband and the bartender were in there.

The group also claims, that during six visits to the hotel, they have witnessed white orbs, cold and hot spots, strange odors, a boy's giggle, and breaking glass in the barroom. While they have found no evidence of "Aggie" or Billy Karsten III, they claim to have photographic evidence of William Karsten, having matched his apparition to a historical photograph. Karsten was a large man, over 350 pounds, with thinning hair and a mustache...rather easy to identify.

Bob observes dress on the wall—
looks a lot like a ghost!

But so much for notes and hearsay—we wanted to document our own experiences. The desk clerk let us investigate vacant rooms on the second floor—nothing "jumped out at us" there. We looked at the diaries in the rooms (noted above).

The front desk clerk took us for a tour of the basement. I speak for myself when I say that we had no uneasy feelings; but, we were startled—not once, but twice! The unfinished basement is divided into a few rooms, most used for storage. Large pipes running the length of the room are visible overhead. At one point, a pipe shook violently and noisily for several seconds; then it stopped. Our "guide" jumped back in surprise and commented, "I've heard that the pipes move when the dishwasher is started, but never expected this force!" This happened again a few minutes later when we came back from our tour to the adjacent rooms.

The desk clerk reached into a barrel and pulled out a handful of wooden nickels--as a souvenir for each of us--actually once used for discounts off pizza or sub sandwiches. (Note: Wooden nickels were first used in the early 1930s as scrip money when a bank failed. This has absolutely nothing to do with this story!)

The desk clerk gives us a tour of the basement.

That night around midnight I lay in my bed alternating between light sleep and sleeplessness. When my eyes were open, they would fixate on the little light on the fire sprinkler in the ceiling--the one that flashes now and then to let you know it is still working. So whether it was my eyes playing tricks on me because I was staring at the flashing light for too long, or whether I had slipped back into a semi-sleep mode, I'm not sure. I do remember thinking what I saw near the top of the wall was something like sheeting northern lights, only they were white. Maybe it was more like a fog. Then the mist floated like a large wide serpent across the top of the wall opposite me, and in a moment it was gone. There is a third option. We *were* in *her* room!

In the morning I answer a knock on our door, still in my pajamas. "Can you come across to our room; we had an "Aggie" visit last night."

Edye proceeds to tell me that she woke up in the middle of the night and smelled very strong floral perfume—sort of like roses. She had hoped for a "materialization" so kept quiet, and nobody else woke up. Then they showed me a tan colored "glob" in the bathroom sink that had a consistency of a liquid makeup, and swore it wasn't there when they went to bed. They affirmed it was not theirs; they don't use makeup of that sort nor did they have any lotion that smelled or looked like that.

We headed downstairs for breakfast, repeating our experiences to anyone who would listen. Everyone was eager to talk with us. Even the restaurant manager shared a few stories. He told of a shelf full of glasses that suddenly crashed to the floor for no apparent reason. It was the middle shelf, sturdy and well supported. Alarm clocks in the kitchen go off at midnight. Salt shakers and sugar bowls are knocked over. Although he didn't know why she would go on a rampage in the kitchen, Agatha gets the blame!

Agatha's apparition has been seen and heard sweeping the halls. Her old-fashioned gray hair pins are sometimes found. One time, while cleaning a mirror, a staff member saw Agatha's apparition appear. She was dressed in a maid uniform; her hair styled in a bun, a popular style of the period.

After breakfast, Tom Schuller, Kewaunee County Historical Society President, stopped by to talk with me. Tom has spent many hours at the hotel doing research--and experiencing his own phenomena!

"One is recurring," he related. "In the north hall on the second floor, there is a 20 foot stretch where I get an eerie feeling and the hair on the back of my neck stands on end." He feels Billy III, who is "stuck in a time warp," runs down this hall to his grandfather's room. There was another incident. "I was just a couple steps down from the first landing when I heard a ball bouncing right next to me." He explained the logic in the episode. The steps were not carpeted back in the 1920s when young Billie was here.

Tom Schuller visits with me in the lobby of the Karsten.

Tom was late for another appointment so he left, and I returned to reading the logs.

56

My ears perked up to a conversation that the maid was having with the desk clerk. I walked over and joined in the chat. The maid had a pillowcase in her hands and explained that she had pulled it from a pillow on Thursday afternoon as she was cleaning a second-floor room. (It is now Saturday morning.) There were only two guests on that floor Wednesday night, and she noticed nothing on the pillowcases from either room as she stripped the bed linens.

Now, after removing them from the dryer, she noticed this elaborate design. It looked as if it had been drawn with a black marker, but it would not rub off. I thought it looked like one of those ink-spot drawings that psychiatrists supposedly use to get ideas on what their patients are thinking! The three of us agreed that at least one of the formations looked like a rose!

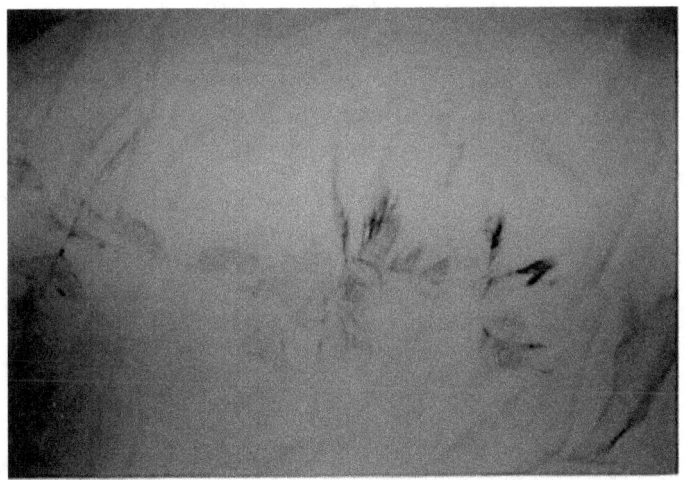

The design on the pillowcase.

William Karsten Sr. died of a heart attack in his suite on January 4, 1940. Young Billie Karsten died of influenza meningitis on February 21, 1940.

Agatha died on July 7, 1954. She is buried in the cemetery up the hill on Ellis Street. But she is not there...she likes it here at The Historic Karsten Inn! Some say that she may be carrying a torch for the senior William Karsten. Don't look for the name "Agatha" on her tombstone; it's not her real name. Her descendents still live in the Kewaunee area and prefer anonymity.

Young Billie still likes to bounce his ball, run down the second floor hallway, and make friends with some of the children of guests staying here.

Did I just hear someone cough? Mr. Karsten used to sit in the lobby—right over there, in his favorite stuffed chair, with his hand curled around a snifter of brandy!!

Note: The hotel closed in June 2007 but reopened in May 2008 doing business as the Kewaunee Inn @ Hamachek Village. The new owners confirm that the hotel is indeed still haunted!

CHAPTER 6

EDYE'S DREAMS

You are not wrong, who deem
That my days have been a dream;
Yet if hope has flown away
In a night, or in a day,
In a vision, or in none,
Is it therefore the less *gone?*
***All* that we see or seem**
Is but a dream within a dream.[6]

For as long as she can remember, Edye Urban has possessed, as they say, a sixth sense. People and events appear to her in her dreams, yet she senses that her vision is actually reality; incidents are really happening and figures in her dreams are real beings, and the two seem to coincide in perfect timing.

Everything appeared as it was, and when it was, in this dream; all, except for the face. There was no face on the woman.

Edye woke with a start and looked at the clock on the table beside the bed. It was 2:30 a.m. Something had happened; she had to wake her husband.

"Urban, wake up!" She had to talk about what happened. "Someone died." They didn't know of anyone who was terminally ill or anyone who had passed away recently. Yet in the vivid dream, Edye

---

[6] From "A Dream Within a Dream," Edgar Allen Poe

envisioned the funeral, the casket--and the faceless woman.

Edye tossed and turned thinking about the dream, but finally drifted back to sleep. In what seemed like a matter of minutes the alarm rang; there was work to be done!

Edye Urban at home in her kitchen near Casco, Wisconsin.

Edye mentioned the dream to co-workers at work. It was a small town; maybe someone could shed light on what this was all about. Nobody could come up with any ideas about who had died.

Edye went on to explain to me the events that followed the dream. "It was the weekend, and we went to this bar where we frequently stopped to see friends. Coincidentally, this man that Urban grew up with was there and came over to talk. The man had been raised by his grandmother, whom he called 'Mom'." Though they were neighbors, Edye had never met the man who lived just down the road from their farm. The man spoke to Urban, "Mom died last night."

The farm where the Urban family lived at the time of the dream.

Urban began asking questions. The man went on to say that he had found his grandmother lying on the floor next to her bed. He continually offered to help get her up and back into bed. She said three times, "I'll be all right." She wanted to stay on the floor, as if moving was too much of an effort at that time.

Then she died...It was exactly like the dream.

The house down the street where the woman died.

The funeral was lovely. The casket, the flowers, the setting—all just as the scene appeared to Edye in her dream. Except for one thing: The woman in the casket had a face.

———

Edye described another dream that she had several years ago.

Her father-in-law was in an advanced stage of lung cancer and was hospitalized at St. Vincent's in Green Bay. He had undergone surgery, but the cancer had spread and there was nothing more the doctors could do. Two or three days after the surgery, he suffered a stroke that paralyzed parts of his body and affected his ability to speak.

It had been about two weeks since the surgery. "Back then," Edye said, "they kept them in the hospital longer than they do now." He seemed to be "hanging in there."

It was early in the morning hours, Edye's turn to be at his bedside. She went on, "The nurse came in and asked me to leave the room because she had to do a procedure of some sort. She told me I should go home and get some sleep."

Edye debated staying at the hospital or driving home. She knew her husband would be here to relieve her in a short while. Also, she *was* quite fatigued. So she drove the thirty miles back to their farm. It was close to 4 a.m. when she collapsed into her bed and drifted into a fitful sleep.

Her father-in-law came to Edye in her dream. He told her that he was going to be leaving. He wanted Edye to know that.

She awoke with a start, jumped out of bed, hastily threw her clothes on, and ran out the door. The half-hour drive back to the hospital seemed to take an eternity.

Running to the elevator, she pushed the button for the third floor. Even the elevator seemed slow this morning.

The family waiting room was right across from the elevator. Urban was there, a bit surprised to see his wife back already. "What are you doing here?" he asked, explaining that they had just bathed his father and were changing his bed.

"Urbie," Edye said, "He's dying."

Together they walked into his room. The nurse was listening through her stethoscope for a heartbeat.

Edye had to try to communicate, on the chance that there might be a trace of cognizance left. She said "We love you, Dad," took his hand and tapped his fingers two times. It was a signal they had used recently since he had been paralyzed by the stroke and unable to speak. He would tap back on her hand the identical number of times.

There was just a slight hesitation. He lightly tapped her finger twice! Then he was gone—he never opened his eyes.

CHAPTER 7

LET SLEEPING BEARS LIE

**When the day is hotly quiet
And the breeze seems not to blow,
One would think the sand was resting
But you'll find this is not so
It is whispering, softly whispering
As it slowly moves along,
And for those who stop and listen
It will sing this mournful song.**[7]

The land *was* quiet then, when the Ojibwa people settled on the eastern shores of Lake Michigan one-half hour west of present-day Traverse City. Golden sand dunes stretch along Lake Michigan's sky-blue waters for 64 miles, comprising the Sleeping Bear Dunes National Lakeshore.

The legend of the Sleeping Bear originated here. As related by a Native American Ojibwa tribal member, the story goes something like this:

Early in the spring of a century long ago, a mother bear named Mishe Mokwa gave birth to two cubs. When the snow melted and the sun shone warm into the entryway of their brushy den, Mother nudged her twins out of their Wisconsin woodland home. During the next weeks the youngsters learned to lap at the ripples of the nearby creek and to search rotten tree stumps for a satiating

---

[7] From *The Shifting Whispering Sands*, V. C. Gilbert

snack of ants and worms. The cubs grew stronger and ever more curious of their surroundings.

Twins in the Pines.

The scorching summer sun soon dried up their water source, and the family made their way down the dry rocky creek bed to the big Lake where they guzzled the cold clear water. Suddenly, menacing dark clouds approached, followed by a terrible storm with lightning and thunder. The frightened baby bears huddled together near the top of the cliff under an overhanging rock, looking to their mother for comfort and assurance that they would not be harmed.

The howling wind pushed the black clouds out over the Lake. The sky grew brighter...and brighter. A large forest fire, fueled by the whipping wind, was soon upon them. Frenzied flames reached skyward as if trying to shake hands with the low-reaching storm clouds. Their forest home was ablaze; there was nowhere for the bears to go. They had fled the forest for lack of water, and now their food source was destroyed as well.

Mother Bear had heard stories of another forestland across the lake. Her healthy young cubs had become good swimmers, so the three began their journey to the distant shore. They swam all day and into the starless night. Mother kept looking back to make sure her cubs were still with her. But the storm persisted and the cubs grew weary. Winds and waves battered the bear family, separating them. Mother was frantic with worry, but clung to the hope that her small cubs were being carried by the elements toward the distant shoreline where she would find them. Her adrenaline pushed her to swim faster toward Michigan...and the safety of the water's edge. Here she would be reunited with her cubs, and the family would find a new home.

But it was not to be. She wandered the miles of beach looking for her cubs. Finally, in desperation, she climbed to the top of the highest bluff that she could find and looked out over the sky-blue waters. Mother Bear never came to accept that both of her cubs had perished in the dark waters. She never left her lookout on the bluff above the lake. In time the Great Spirit Manido brought her up to the spirit world to be reunited with her loving children. Manido (Manitou) was so pleased with the virtues and values of the bear family that he decided a memorial would be appropriate.

He placed a 450-foot pile of sand atop a bluff resembling Mother Bear. Today, the dune is a rounded mound less than 100 feet high. It is expected that in the future erosion will completely eradicate Mother Bear from the bluff, but her spirit and the legend will forever remain. Manido created two islands, North Manitou and South Manitou where the cubs' bodies were pulled from the water.

Trail to the top of the Dunes.

North Manitou, or "Big Bear Island," is about an hour's ride on the ferry from Leland, Michigan. There are old orchards, abandoned cottages and farmland along the east side of the island near the ferry docks, but the interior of the 15,000-acre island is mostly wilderness. The northernmost portion of the island is the most primitive, bordered by 300-foot bluffs with magnificent views of the Lake.

South Manitou Island, is 90 minutes away from the mainland. Here visitors can camp, hike, picnic on quiet beaches, swim in clear water, explore the lighthouse and one-room schoolhouse. The world's largest white cedar tree grows on the southern shore, estimated to be around 500 years old. It is 80 feet tall with a circumference of 17-1/2 feet. Off the south shore, you can view the hull of the Francisco Morazon, a Liberian freighter grounded in 1960.

Sleeping Bear Dunes National Lakeshore.

At the Visitor Center you can learn of the mid-nineteenth-century Hutzler-Riker farm where high-yield Rosen rye was developed. George Johann Hutzler, a German immigrant, was the first settler on the island. Windows of the house owned by Hutzler are boarded up now because a ghost appeared in a window and scared hikers passing by.

The deep harbor at South Manitou was a key refueling station in the mid 1830s for ships heading through the Straits of Mackinac down to Chicago. Many were filled with European immigrants, seeking a better life in America. One particular ship, carrying families from Ireland and Germany was overcrowded to the point where sanitary issues developed. Drinking water became contaminated and dysentery spread throughout the ship. Other passengers developed cholera. The ship was becoming filled with corpses!

The desperate captain spotted South Manitou Island through the fog, and set anchor in the harbor. That night, while waiting to refuel in the morning, crew members dug a mass shallow grave at the edge of the woods adjacent to the beach. Bodies were placed in their final resting place, covered only with a bit of that shifting, whispering sand.

George Hutzler's own son died of cholera on his way to America. Perhaps his spirit is the one that scared the hikers!

The landscape changes quickly and dramatically at Sleeping Bear Dunes. Landslides carry tons of earth into Lake Michigan. "Ghost forests" remain where stately pines once grew. As the westerly wind whips over the dunes, swirling, shifting sand comes to rest against the base of the trees. As more and more sand builds up over the years, the trees will completely disappear from view.

Find a place to rest; sit down. Look out over Lake Michigan; enjoy the beauty and the serenity. And, listen very closely, because

> **If you want to learn the secret**
> **Wander through these quiet lands**
> **And I'm sure you'll hear the story**
> **Of the shifting, whispering sands.**[8]

---

[8] From *The Shifting Whispering Sands*, V. C. Gilbert

CHAPTER 8

SNAKES IN THE WAKE

**Beyond the shadow of the ship,
I watched the water–snakes:
They moved in tracks of shining white,
And when they reared, the elfish light
Fell off in hoary flakes[9]**

Enormous sea (and lake) serpents have surfaced all over the world in the form of multi-humped whales, giant otters with tails, alligators with scales and other forms of cryptozoic sea creatures that live somewhere beneath the surface of large bodies of water. Earlier reports often told of horse-like creatures. The stories of later years seem to resemble a creature more like a reptile or dinosaur.

Many of the stories are from the Great Lakes. Lake Michigan has been the source of many reported sightings dating back to the mid 19th century.

Frederick Stonehouse, in his book "Haunted Lakes II" quotes an archived article from the *Chicago Tribune:*

> That Lake Michigan is inhabited by a vast monster, part fish and part serpent, no longer admits of doubt. We have already published the fact that the crews of the tug *George W. Wood* and the propeller *Sky Lark* had seen

---

[9] From *The Rime of the Ancient Mariner*, Samuel Taylor Coleridge

him off Evanston, lashing the waves into a tempest.

Persons aboard the two ships described the serpentine creature as about 50 feet long and having a girth the size of a barrel.

Commercial fishermen reported sightings of a similar creature in the early 1900s near Milwaukee. Then recreational boaters saw *it*. In the 1930s, people on the Michigan Street Bridge saw the gray-green serpentine animal slowly cruising down the Milwaukee River. Later that day the creature was spotted at the mouth of the river, heading out into Lake Michigan.

A fisherman, described by people who knew him well as "completely honest," experienced a similar sighting on a later date. Despite calm winds, his fishing boat began to rock. Before he caught glimpse of the creature, he heard a noise he described as "half puffing like a heavy breath, and half an actual vocal sound, harsh and grating...." and loud! Turning toward the sound, he saw the creature submerge: "...a bluish-black animal with fins, spines, a very large tail and two well developed legs toward the back of the body," and probably another two front legs that would enable it to walk on the bottom of the lake in search of prey.

Several years prior to the Chicago and Milwaukee sightings, a UFO (unidentified *floating* object) was spotted in Lake Leelanau, just northwest of Traverse City, Michigan. Prior to a dam being built at the outlet of the lake in the late 1800s, water flowed naturally down into Lake Michigan. By the same token, creatures could have made their way up the river and into the lake—where they would have become trapped once the dam was constructed. A local fisherman tied his boat to one of the dead cedar trees sticking out of the water. At that instant, as the story is told, "two eyes opened up, just about face level, or four feet above water, and looked directly at him." The creature quickly submerged and swam off. The fisherman "could see the head past the rear of the boat wile the tail was still in front" of him. Though others in the area came forth with their own stories after this incident was reported, no sightings have occurred in Lake Leelanau for many years. It can be assumed that the creature may have been a lone resident who long since perished.

Fossil whalebones from finback, sperm and right whales have been discovered throughout Michigan on land once covered by water, and whale teeth turn up on beaches. One hypothesis is that the whales got there by swimming up the St. Lawrence or the Hudson channels and eventually into more shallow rivers where they became stranded on beaches along Lake Michigan.

Carbon dating of samples from whale bones here indicate the whales to be 190 to 690 years old, advancing a theory that land in this region emerged from the sea in relatively recent years.

After U. S. Navy vessels spotted a monster while on a training mission in the spring of 2008, they reportedly captured what was described as an intelligent 35-ton, 140-foot dinosaur-like creature with gills and lungs, capable of living in or out of water. Supposedly, the Navy has kept this very quiet and refused to comment because "national security interests may be at stake."

Who knows? Photoshop plus a creative writer....

Many believe that it is possible that the enormous creatures believed to inhabit Lake Michigan today evolved from whales or other, even older, species of mammals or fishes? It literally is a *deep, dark* mystery!

Serpent sighting gives an eerie f EEL i n g.

CHAPTER 9

GHOSTS HAVE FUN IN CHESTERTON

To sit on rocks, to muse o'er flood and fell,
To slowly trace the forest's shady scene,
Where things that own
not man's dominion dwell,
And mortal foot hath ne'er or rarely been...
This to be alone; this, this is solitude![10]

Chesterton is a growing community of over 13,000 people located about twenty miles from Gary, Indiana, half way between the Illinois and Michigan borders. Chesterton is home to the Indiana Dunes State Park, established in 1923. In 1966 The Indiana Dunes National Lakeshore was established. Future land acquisitions added to both parks and to the significance of Chesterton.

Check out various web sites on the internet. There are stories of happenings near Ghost Road in Chesterton, haunted by a group of demented people who attacked and killed people years ago. Further down the road people have seen a woman surrounded in a bluish light. Some see her sitting in a rocking chair in the field where once her house stood. The house burned down over 100 years ago, and her son perished in the fire. Others see her darting in and out of the nearby woods looking for her son, as she did that night of the fire. At least one

---

[10] From *Solitude*, Lord Byron.

person has felt the presence of the boy near the fire scene.

Another person tells of an incident that occurred in the family home in the woods outside of Chesterton. The family's dogs, normally quiet, began barking inside the house. They sounded terrified, yet acted very protective. Later that night they started growling again, facing a particular corner. Then, this person saw a vision of a woman dressed in a white gown floating through the wall by that corner!

Back in October 1933 a United Airlines twin-engine passenger plane travelling from Cleveland to Chicago exploded over Chesterton killing three crew members and four passengers. A nitro-glycerin explosive device was discovered among the wreckage, documenting the first known case of airline sabotage.

A local pizzeria supposedly is haunted by a former owner. The Porter County Home burned down years ago, but ghosts of the residents there still linger. In addition, Chesterton IS home to the "Indiana Ghost Trackers" organization.

This story, however, takes place along the Indiana Dunes National Lakeshore, and is about a woman dubbed "Diana of the Dunes."

In Greek mythology Artemis, also known as Diana, was the daughter of the mighty Zeus, ruler of the Olympian gods, and his wife, Leto. After a painful childbirth, Leto grew very weak. As legend has it, several hours after her own delivery Artemis assisted her mother in the birth of her twin brother Apollo! Thus goddess Artemis (Diana) continued into her life as a nurturer and protector.

Diana came to be known as a protector of children...and the environment. She was a pioneer feminist—independent, decisive, and born to be free! Although considerate of gentle animals, Diana was a fearless huntress who brought down many predators with her bow and arrows. Diana never married and, in fact, had only one serious love affair. Her twin, Apollo, jealous of his twin sister's attention to her lover Orion, challenged Diana to shoot an arrow at a distant object in the ocean. Diana hit her mark. Unbeknownst to Diana, the "object" she shot was Orion, out for a long swim!

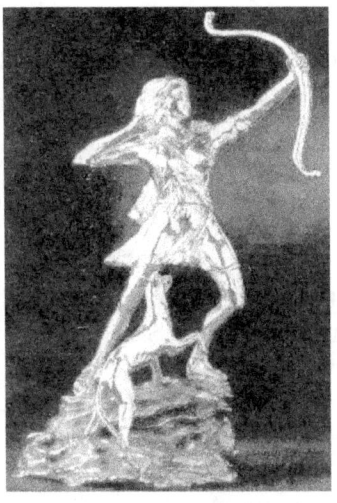

Statue of Huntress Diana.

Absorbed in overwhelming grief, and extreme anger at Apollo, Diana suddenly came up with a brilliant idea. She quickly turned Orion into a star and then shot him high into the sky with her trusty bow. He still remains in the heavens, shining brightly among the multitude of twinkling stars. Today, the constellation, Orion, is familiar to all stargazers.

Alice Marble Gray was born in 1881 into an influential and wealthy family in Chicago, Illinois. As a child, Alice traveled with her parents throughout the Midwest. One of their favorite places was the quiet, wooded area where they came to relax. That area is now Indiana Dunes State Park.

She entered the University of Chicago at age 16, studying math, astronomy, Greek and Latin. Upon graduation as a Phi Beta Kappa with honors, she was employed as a computer operator at the U. S. Naval Observatory for about two years

Perhaps a bit bored with her job, Alice left the Observatory to attend the University of Gottinger in Germany. It was here that she joined *Wandervogel*, also known as *Birds of Passing*, a "walking commune" that promoted young people to give up their material possessions and live as one with nature.

Upon her return to Chicago, Alice worked for an astronomy magazine. She was well traveled, independent and self-reliant. Those qualities, plus her love for nature, were similar to those of Artemis (Diana).

"In solitude when we are least alone," a passage from Lord Byron's poem, *Solitude*, inspired Alice to finally "give up the conventional world" and move to the remote and mainly uninhabited Dunes in 1915. Gray was quoted in the *Chicago Examiner* in July 1916:

> I wanted to live my own life--a free life. The life of a salary earner in the cities is slavery, a constant fight for the means of living. Here it is so different. My salary when I worked was nothing extraordinary, and yet here I have lived all winter and summer on the last pay envelope

that I received in Chicago. I buy only bread and salt. When I came here in October, 1915, I had nothing but a jelly glass, a knife, a spoon, a blanket and two guns. For four nights before discovering this abandoned hut, I slept under the stars. Then I began housekeeping, and all the furniture I have is made of driftwood.

Alice lived in an abandoned 10'x10' windowless fisherman's shack that she named "Driftwood," with her few belongings. She pored over books from a local library, walked the beach, and swam in the invigorating Lake Michigan. Some say she continued her interest in astronomy by studying the effects of the moon on the tides.

The Dunes were her dream, a place where she could be free. She would promote preservation of the beautiful area that she had come to love during her childhood visits. She lectured, gave tours to children, and wrote about her passion. Alice lived off the land and the lake, eating fish, wild game, berries and plants. Her meager income came from the sale of her driftwood boxes—and perhaps berries and wild game as well.

Fishermen often caught a glimpse of the attractive woman swimming in the nude as the sun set over the lake. Chicago newspapers reporters repeatedly dogged her and wrote negatively about her free existence.

Alice became recognized as a superior huntress. A story in the November 1916 *Chesterton Tribune* gave her the nickname "Diana," after the newspaper reporters observed a number of ducks hanging from a line beside her cabin. They felt that she possessed many of the same traits as the Greek woodland goddess Diana. From that time on Alice began to be referred to as "Diana." Her small cabin was located somewhere northwest of the intersection of Highways 12 and 49 just outside of Indiana Dunes State Park, close to Porter.

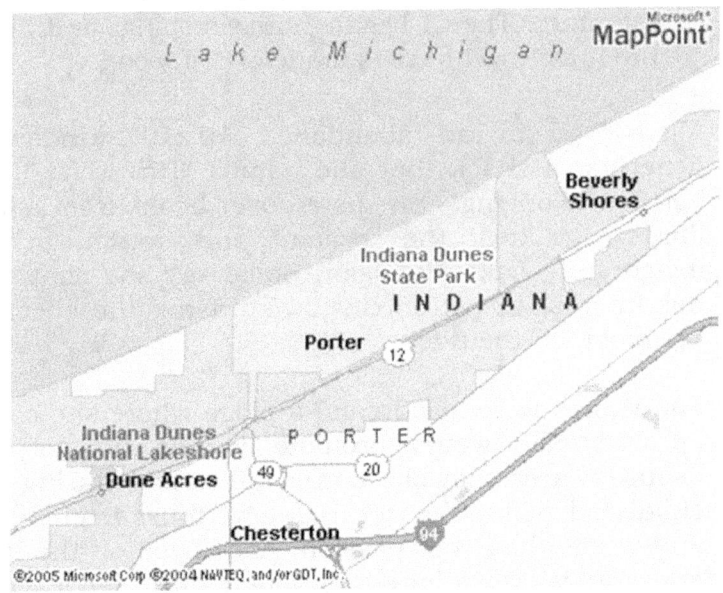

Map showing the area of Diana's home.

About five years after moving to the Dunes, Alice met and fell in love with an unemployed carpenter, Paul Eisenblatter (aka Paul Wilson), a drifter with a somewhat questionable past. Reporters referred to the 6' 5" man as the "Giant of the Dunes."

Before long the couple moved to another shack they named "Wrens Nest," just a few miles east of "Driftwood." There are varying reports about their life together, but a common thread seems to be that Paul continued to have problems with the law and that he physically abused Alice. At one point Alice was hospitalized with a skull injury from a fight that broke out when a boatman brought several curiosity seekers to see where "Diana of the Dunes" lived. Wilson, jealous of Alice, supposedly started the fight. He was shot in the foot.

A man was murdered in 1922 and discovered on the beach close to the couple's home. Police questioned Wilson as a suspect, but did not have enough evidence to hold him.

Despite the turmoil in their life, the couple had two daughters together. Not much is known about the daughters or what happened to them after the fateful day of February 11, 1925 when police found Alice's body on the beach near "Wren's Nest." Again, Wilson was arrested, but was released for lack of substantial evidence. Some accounts say Alice died of uremia poisoning, yet there was evidence of blows to her back and her stomach.

It was here at the Dunes where Alice felt as free as the wind and as strong as the waves crashing onto the shore. She loved the area; many said that she wished her ashes to be scattered over the Dunes. Other reports said that she wanted to be buried in her private family cemetery. Despite her wishes, her body was carried away from the spot where she gasped her last breath and laid to rest in an unmarked grave at Oak Lawn Cemetery in Gary, Indiana.

As for Wilson, the local newspaper reported that he was arrested at Alice's funeral when he threatened to kill a newspaperman with a pistol. The following year Wilson allegedly married another woman, was arrested during a highway hold-up, and later killed during another robbery.

Alice never really left the Dunes. Her spirit still roams the land she always felt was her true home. Over the years many have seen a wispy figure of the naked woman running free along the sun-warmed beach and splashing into Lake Michigan's cool blue waters.

A transparent figure emerges from the lake.

Today The Diana of the Dunes Festival and Pageant is held yearly in Chestertown, Indiana to honor Alice Gray and raise funds for non-profit organizations in the area.

Mention Diana of the Dunes in the Chesterton area, and the old-timers there will gladly take the time to tell you a tale, probably passed down and around once or twice...but nevertheless interesting and intriguing.

CHAPTER 10

BLOOD MOON RISING

**The Wendigos walk with the gods of wind
and they are not the friends of men.
When you expect them least of all,
they race the waves in a sudden squall...[11]**

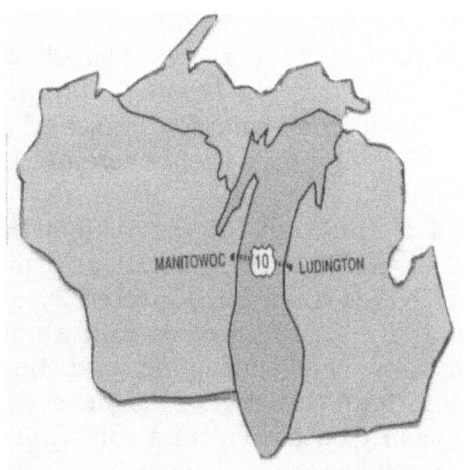

Route of the S. S. Badger.

First Mate Colyn McGruder moved quickly along the rows of cars and trucks that lined deck B of the car ferry S.S. Badger. He was well ahead of his schedule and, this being the midnight run, there were only about half as many vehicles as earlier in the day. He paused momentarily to tug on a rear strap that secured the back of the Jeep Grand Cherokee to the

---

[11] From *Blood Moon*, Robert W. Sandlin, Jr.

deck. "Probably a waste of time," he thought to himself as he tightened the ratchet several clicks. The Coast Guard weather channel had called for westerly winds at three to five knots per hour and chop at less than two feet. For Lake Michigan that was as smooth as glass.

Lake Michigan Ferry

"But I've told these kids a hundred times
Don't take the Lakes for granted.
They go from calm to a hundred knots
So fast they seem enchanted."

The words to the Stan Rogers' tune *White Squall* ran through his mind...a song about an iron ore ship on the Great Lakes that encountered one of the freak storms that the inland sailors talk about. Colyn had never actually seen one (nor had he ever known anyone who had) but then, he'd never known anyone who had seen God either yet a lot of folks believed in his (or her) existence.

Before he knew it, he was humming the tune to the song as he moved along the cars. Suddenly the song caught in his throat, replaced by a slow exhalation of breath. He stopped dead in his tracks and stared in disbelief. At the head of the line of vehicles was the most beautiful sight he had ever seen. A 1940 CV75 Cadillac roadster. Its dull fire-engine-red finish seemed to gleam in the iridescent lower-deck lighting.

"What maniac would actually drive this automobile?"
He was speaking out loud and his incredulous voice echoed off the steel bulkheads of the ship. But what he had said was true. Something like this should be in a glass case somewhere in Detroit, if not the Smithsonian. In fact, given the condition it was in, Colyn wasn't so sure that the Institute wasn't where it came from. Certainly it didn't belong strapped to the pitching deck of a car ferry on its way to Ludington, Michigan! He wanted to go immediately to his room and check it out on his computer. Certainly a car like this had to be registered with the auto clubs out of Michigan. Maybe he could even locate the owners on board. What if he could talk them into a ride when the ferry arrived in Michian?!

"Right," he thought, "Hop right into my million dollar collector's car, Mr. McGruder. Would you like to drive?!!"

His reverie was interrupted by the ship's intercom, "Mr. McGruder dial the bridge...Mr. McGruder dial the bridge please." It was Captain Lawford's voice. The magic Caddy would have to wait.

"McGruder here Captain," he responded as the Captain picked up the intercom.

"Where are you, Number One," the skipper asked. There seemed to be an edge to his voice.

"B deck, sir," the First Mate snapped, "Phone station number 4."

"Report to the bridge as soon as you finish inspecting the racks."

"I'm on my way Captain." McGruder latched the phone down and headed toward the gangway that would take him to the crew ladder and the main deck.

The well-polished deck of the S.S. Badger reflected the moonlight. She wasn't a young ship, commissioned in the early fifties. She was a veteran of the Lakes, but very well maintained. McGruder was into his fifth year aboard, and he really loved his work. It brought together the two loves of his life--ships and cars. Colyn glanced up at the half moon. There was a faint ring outlining both the lit and dark halves and, to Colyn, it almost appeared to be a faint red.

"First Mate McGruder reporting, sir," Colyn sounded as he entered the bridge.

"Relax Colyn," the Captain smiled, "Just us old salts up here for now. Coffee?"

"Thank you, Captain," McGruder smiled back, "You sounded a little anxious on the squawk."

"You check the moon on the way up?" The Captain looked at him over the rim of his cup.

"Red ring?" Colyn remarked, making sure not even a hint of the smile about what he was thinking showed on his face.

"I'm sure your old man told you 'bout a "blood moon.'" The Captain was dead serious.

"Yes sir," Colyn replied, "He did; but he also sailed under them."

"And how did that turn out?" the Captain's voice was taking on that edge again.

"He never went into it," McGruder said truthfully, "and I never asked."

"Well," Lawford sighed, "We'll sail under it as well, but by God I don't have to like it! Sound general quarters and make ready to get under way, number one."

"Aye-Aye, sir," McGruder snapped. He flipped the intercom switch and summoned all hands to prepare for disembarking. One by one the stations reported in and the Captain ordered the engines up. With a roar the Badger's twin 1200 horsepower diesels sprang to life. With two short and one long blast the ship eased her berth and slid across the black water of Manitowoc harbor, towards the breakwater and the open arms of Lake Michigan.

They were well past the harbor marker now, making eighteen knots in six hundred and fifty some feet of water.

"That will be all for now Mr. McGruder," Captain Lawford said, "You can return to your duties. Keep a sharp eye tonight and mind the 'blood moon.' Send Two Thumbs around with some hot coffee when he's a mind." The Captain was referring to Charley Swenson, the ship's cook, whom everyone referred to as Two Thumbs.

"Aye Cap'n," Colyn responded on his way out the door.

He glanced up again at the half moon descending now towards the stern of the Badger. It appeared to Colyn that the red ring was even more pronounced. He was glad Captain Lawford couldn't see towards the stern without leaving the wheelhouse.

McGruder wondered how seriously the Captain of the S.S. Badger took the old legends of the Lakes. If he was anything like Colyn's father, the First Mate was glad he had been able to suppress the smile!

Back in the crew's mess Two Thumbs was on his hands and knees wiping up the tile floor.

"What's up, Charley?" McGruder questioned.

"Dropped the stew," Charley said, not bothering to look up.

Colyn looked at Frank Kupper who was seated against the bulkhead and Chelsey Bourne in the chair next to him. They both smiled at the First Mate as if to say, *"Hey...why do you think we call him Two Thumbs?"*

How are things up top?" Frank asked referring to the wheelhouse.

"Smooth," Colyn said. He spoke to Charley, "Cap'n would like some hot coffee when you got time."

"I'm all over it," Charley said.

"Did you notice the blood moon?" Frank asked Colyn.

"Not you too," Colyn said wearily, "I'd think a third year engineering major from Michigan Tech would have more to occupy his mind than Indian ghost stories."

"Don't be so quick to pass off our ancient lore, white man," Two Thumbs said, feigning being offended.

"Sorry 'Little Big Man'," Colyn shot back, "I forgot you were, what...from the Norwegian band of the Ojibwa Nation?"

Charley looked up with a big grin on his face. "The Wendigo will get you for that," he winked at the First Mate.

"What is all this stuff about a 'blood moon'?" Chelsey queried. "Half the crew is muttering about it. Sorry, I must have missed a chapter in my 'old salts training manual'."

"Well my child," Charley said, pulling himself up from the floor and plopping into a chair at the table, "It's not so much a sailor story as it is Ojibwa lore. As my Grandmother, Little Song Bird, used to tell the story..."

"Oh please," Colyn pretended to choke on his coffee, "*Little Song Bird?*" Your grandmother's name is Swenson, just like yours, and you're about as much Native American as Lutefisk!"

"Pay no attention to the bigot at the head of the table," Charley sniffed his disgust, "He will, undoubtedly, be dead by morning. My Indian blood comes from my mother's side of the family."

Chelsey and Frank laughed, Charley and Colyn carried on this good-natured harangue constantly. Charley continued with his narrative... "The Ojibwa worshipped a number of gods including the gods of wind and fire."

"Yeah," said Colyn dryly, "and they eventually joined up with the god of earth and formed a rock band. You guys remember *Earth, Wind and Fire*...right?"

Two Thumbs shot Colyn a look he usually reserved to make sour cream. "You're going to get very hungry before we reach Ludington white boy," he said, and then continued:

The Wind gods and the Thunder gods were enemies and they would often battle above the Great Lakes. The Wind gods weren't as strong as the Thunder gods so they relied on surprise and trickery. One trick they particularly liked was to becalm the air and water and then suddenly strike out as a raging storm out of nowhere...a white squall. However, because the Wind gods were also the gods of Fire, their presence was always given away by a red glow...like the one around the moon tonight.

Suddenly an old sea shanty that his father had often sung came into Colyn's head. Muttering more to himself than those seated at the table, he chanted it softly.

Beware the Lakes when the moon wears red
And the winds go calm and the waves lie dead.
Pay heed to the wind gods, it is said
The white squalls rage when the moon wears red.[12]

McGruder looked around the table and everyone was staring at him.

"Not bad whitey," Charley snorted, "throw in a flute, and you can appear at the next pow-wow."

"Take the Captain some hot coffee, Tonto," Colyn smiled at his friend, "and don't call him 'Kemosabe'. He hates it when you do that."

Colyn was on his computer searching out vintage Cadillacs when the intercom beside his bunk buzzed. "McGruder here," Colyn responded.

---

[12] From *Blood Moon*, Robert W. Sandlin Jr.

"I need you on the bridge," Captain Lawford said tersely.

"Aye, sir," Colyn replied, "five minutes."

"Make it four," the Captain said and hung up. Colyn made it in three but he was breathing hard.

"I received a short transmission from the Heartland," Lawford began without waiting for Colyn to acknowledge reporting in. The Heartland was a Coast Guard cutter out of Benton Harbor, Michigan. "She encountered a white squall 165 degrees, six minutes and 22 miles outside Benton. Coast Guard now advises all vessels to take precautionary measures for unexpected weather conditions. Damn the blood moon anyway!"

"Very good captain," Colyn said as he flipped on the intercom.

"Attention ship's crew and station supervisors...rig for a Level 3 weather alert. Repeat...Alert Level 3 is now in effect." The warning told the crew that rough weather was expected and passengers should be inside at all times. All crewmembers outside the ship were required to wear lifelines and life jackets.

Next Colyn consulted the Loran guidance system and G.P.S. coordinates. The Badger was ten minutes from the midway point between Ludington and Manitowoc and just inside the *Lake Michigan Triangle*. The 'triangle' was another Great Lakes myth though not as old as the 'blood moon.' The triangle ran from Ludington to Benton Harbor, crossed the lake to Manitowoc and ran back to Ludington. Like the Bermuda triangle (from whence came the name), this area had more than its share of unexplained mysteries. Ships had disappeared without a trace and their electrical equipment and compasses reacted strangely when inside the 'triangle.'

"We're in the soup, aren't we?" Captain Lawford asked.

"Sorry Captain." McGruder looked up from the charts, "I never believed all that bilge about blood moons and triangles. I do believe in freak storms and rogue waves, but I don't think they are sent by Ojibwa gods or the boogey man."

"You're entitled to believe what you want Number One," the old man smiled as he replied, "I felt the same way...once."

Suddenly the marine band radio crackled to life, "Mayday...mayday...mayday...Sea Witch out of Benton Harbor calling mayday...mayday...mayday."

McGruder and Captain Lawford both hesitated, certain that the Coast Guard Cutter Heartland would respond. Fifteen seconds passed, then twenty, and once more the mayday distress call was repeated. Colyn moved first to grab the microphone.

"Sea Witch...Sea Witch...Sea Witch...This is S.S. Badger. We copy your mayday. State your situation and location, over." There were a few seconds of silence and then...

"Badger...Badger...Badger this is Sea Witch. Thank God! We are capsized in high seas. Last position at G.P.S. latitude 44 degrees, 14 minutes, 30 seconds north; longitude 29 degrees, 40 minutes, eight seconds west...do you copy?"

Colyn keyed the mike as he plotted the chart, "We copy Sea Witch, stand by." Two quick pencil lines and some very fast figuring with the G.P.S. and Colyn called to the captain, "She's 2.25 miles off our starboard bow, sir. Come to heading 110 degrees, 12 minutes."

Again Colyn keyed the mike, "We have you, Sea Witch, and are proceeding your position. ETA (estimated time of arrival) is fifteen minutes. Do you copy?"

"Hurry Badger," was the only answer and then dead air. Colyn tried twice to raise the stricken ship without success. His second attempt was interrupted by the Heartland. Badger...Badger...Badger...this is Coast Guard Cutter Heartland, do you copy?"

"Heartland this is Badger, go ahead," Colyn responded.

"Badger," Heartland called, "we have you on frequency two-niner-zero. Who are you *pinging* (responding to)? Over."

"We have a mayday from vessel Sea Witch reporting as capsized in heavy seas," Colyn responded. "We are proceeding to her position." Colyn gave Heartland the last position he had received from the Sea Witch.

"We did not receive Sea Witch," the Heartland reported, "Strange...we have your signal five by five. We are also proceeding to her position from the south. E.T.A. eighteen minutes...Heartland out."

Now there were two ships responding to the mayday call. Colyn stepped outside the Bridge. The night sky was brilliantly clear with the red-circled moon now close to the horizon off their starboard beam. The Lake appeared perfectly calm in the white path of the moonlight. He stepped back inside and dialed the security station on the intercom. Frank Kupper answered, and Colyn quickly filled him in on the situation. He then ordered a rescue team to the starboard side of the ship. They would make ready a lifeboat in the event that the Badger was first on the scene.

"Ten minutes out," Captain Lawford told his executive officer, "better man the forward light."

Colyn already had a life jacket strapped on. Outside the bridge a steel cable ran around the side of the ship parallel to the walkway. Colyn attached a nylon chord from his life jacket to the cable. This was his lifeline and it would be his only hope if he lost his footing while on deck. He made his way to the bow of the ship where a powerful one-million-candlepower searchlight was mounted.

The intense white orb skimmed across two-foot waves some thirty feet below. A two-foot sea was a placid surface for Lake Michigan. The blood moon had finally gone to rest past the horizon, and there seemed to be a haze blanketing all but the brightest stars. The night was ink black at the bow of the S.S. Badger. The buzz of the intercom at the bow light station made Colyn jump. It was Captain Lawford. "We are closing in on your chart point Number One," he informed the First Mate, "Keep a sharp eye; the life boat team is standing by on the starboard side." "Aye, sir," Colyn responded.

His search beam showed nothing as it danced across the glistening surface of Michigan's skin. The verses from his father's old shanty, "The Blood Moon" were echoing in his mind...

And suddenly the Lake rose high
With waves that lashed the midnight sky,

With winds that screamed like the eagle's cry.
Before such fury courage flies. [13]

They were now right on top of the coordinates given them by the stricken vessel *Sea Witch* but the flood lights and search beam showed no signs of wreckage or debris. The inky depths of Lake Michigan were calm and silent...almost like a tomb. The squawk beside the light station sprang to life...making Colyn jump.

"Report, Number One," Captain Lawford ordered.

"I don't see a sign of...." McGruder's voice was lost in the roar.

It struck with the savagery of a coiled snake, full of energy from the first instant. There was no warning. One instant Colyn was facing starboard with the search beam on the water...the next he was stretched toward port at the end of his lifeline. A gale wind ripped at his face, threatening to remove his eyebrows. Icy water slashed across his exposed flesh like millions of tiny razor blades. He could hear nothing but the *screaming of eagles* as he felt the Badger listing hard to port. A thirty foot wave broke over the starboard rail...and then another. Colyn thought that his torso might tear apart as it strained against the tethered life jacket strapped to his chest. His frozen fingers found the searchlight mount and gripped it with all his strength. If the nylon lifeline snapped, he was a dead man.

"Another ten degrees of list," he thought, "and the ship will certainly roll." In a flash of thought he said farewell to everyone he knew and in that instant...it ended!

---

[13] From *Blood Moon,* Robert W. Sandlin Jr.

Like a wet and angry dog the Badger shook herself and rolled upright again. Colyn staggered and leaned against the searchlight mounting. The light itself was completely missing, ripped from its steel bracket and tossed into the sea. Colyn absent-mindedly fingered the now slack lifeline that dangled from his dripping life jacket. His brain was just not functioning, but at a deeper level he understood how lucky he was to still be alive.

The Lake was silent. The coiled snake had struck and slithered off into the darkness, leaving everything the way it had been...when? How long ago? Was it hours... minutes... seconds? Colyn realized the answer. It had been a lifetime ago. Like all those sailors who had lived through a 'white squall,' his life would never be the same again. He had no idea how long he stood at the bow in a daze but the sound of running feet and the shouting of his name brought him back to the moment. It was Frank and Two Thumbs in life jackets and lines. They carried dry blankets and a first aid kit, but it soon became obvious that they had had little hope of needing either.

"God almighty he's alive!" Frank yelled, "I can't believe you're alive!"

The huge six-foot, six-inch Finlander and Charley both grabbed Colyn in bear hugs, one on either side of him.

"Obviously the Wind Gods don't want a white bigot in their midst," Charley laughed but he made no attempt to disguise the tears that glistened in his dark eyes.

"Cap'n Lawford didn't give much hope that you survived up here," Frank said as he wrapped the blanket around Colyn's shivering shoulders, "but Two

Thumbs told him it would take more than Indian folk lore to do you in."

Colyn looked thoughtfully at his shipmate Two Thumbs. "You were almost wrong," he said softly, "no more jokes about Indians or their folk lore...ever. And I want to meet your grandmother--what's her name again?"

"Oh," Charley grinned, "you mean 'Little Song Bird'? Actually, her name is Beatrice...Beatrice Swenson. I'll introduce you the next time we're in Iola, Wisconsin. Maybe you can come to the Lutefisk festival."

Then all three of them were laughing as they headed back to the bridge to relieve Captain Lawford's anxiety. Suddenly a loud clap of thunder split the silence of the Lake Michigan night as it rolled across the black water.

"Ah," Charley said, glancing to the north, "the Thunder Gods are answering the challenge of the Wind Gods. The Thunder Gods always win you know." He seemed to be waiting for a smart remark from his friend Colyn. This time there was none.

CHAPTER 11

SCALENE SCENE

**The night, though clear, shall frown,
And the stars shall not look down
From their high thrones in the Heaven...**[14]

If the stars did look down over the *Triangle,* they might be confused, dismayed, frightened, and even angered. For here, beneath their beams of light, an atmosphere of mystery merges with the dark cold waters of Lake Michigan. Here, mortal men have descended to a frigid grave far beneath the Lake's surface.

You've heard of a mathematical triangle, love triangle, the Bermuda Triangle...but did you know that there is a Lake Michigan Triangle? (You probably do now, if you read the last chapter carefully!)

There is an area bordered by a perimeter running from Ludington, Michigan, south to Benton Harbor, and then across the lake to Manitowoc, Wisconsin and back to Ludington, forming an outline of a scalene triangle. Within this triangle strange objects and living beings appear and disappear. Sea creatures have been spotted here, so have unidentified flying objects (UFOs). Large vessels like the steamship Alpena that disappeared in 1880, as well as small sailboats and excursion boats, have vanished suddenly and permanently. Ghost planes have

---

[14] From *Spirits of the Dead,* Edgar Allan Poe

appeared as false images on radar screens at O'Hare International Airport and the Terminal Radar Approach Control Center in Elgin, Illinois. In spring 2000, an estimated 130 such images appeared within a five-week period.

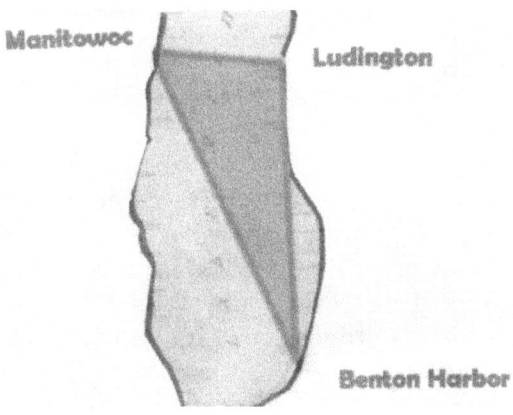

Lake Michigan Triangle

Ships

Let's begin when the strange incidents began to be reported. At 9:30 p.m. on Friday, October 15, 1880 the 197-foot wooden steamer *Alpena* left Grand Haven, Michigan, bound for Chicago. (Grand Haven is located approximately half way between Ludington and Benton Harbor.)

The weather was beautiful, warm and calm, but by 3 a.m. on Saturday a storm called the "worst gale in Lake Michigan recorded history" hit with a fury. A few hours later the *Alpena* was spotted by other vessels about 35 miles offshore from Kenosha, Wisconsin. What happened after that is speculation, but reports indicate the steamer probably capsized and was blown back close to the Michigan lakeshore when it sank late Saturday or early Sunday. An estimated 80 people perished. Debris floated onto beaches at

99

Holland, Michigan (located about 25 miles south of Ludington.)

About ten carloads of apples were stowed on deck. Some believe that a shift in cargo during the storm may have caused the ship to sink. Thousands of apples were found bobbing in the water several miles south of Holland.

Another ship, a three-mast schooner named the *Rouse Simmons*, disappeared as it was about to enter the *Triangle* just north of Manitowoc. Known as the "Christmas Tree Ship," the vessel was headed from Manistique, Michigan, on its way to Chicago fully loaded with bundles of fragrant pine and balsam trees. Tree farms in Wisconsin and Michigan were buried with snow, so the tree cargo would yield a handsome profit upon delivery. While not the only ship carrying such cargo, the *Rouse Simmons* was the only one to sell directly to the public, thus avoiding the middleman.

Launched in 1868 and named after a Kenosha, Wisconsin man (one of three who financed the venture), the 244-ton, 124-foot *Rouse Simmons* was a fine ship in its time. But by the time of what would prove to be its last journey, the vessel was described by some as "rickety and ramshackled." That fact, plus perhaps the overconfidence of a seasoned and storm-worn skipper, may have precipitated the last voyage of the Christmas-tree ship.

The weather was stormy when the schooner set sail midday on November 25, 1912. The gale intensified overnight, and winds reached speeds of 60 mph. At some point, the schooner took on a huge wave, sweeping two sailors overboard along with several bundles of trees and a small boat. The Captain regained control and maneuvered towards a sheltered cove near Bailey's Harbor, Wisconsin. But the winds quickly changed direction and the ship was blown off its course. Temperatures dropped, and a sudden snowstorm battered the *Rouse Simmons*. Water entering the hold froze onto the trees and added more weight to a ship that already was carrying a heavy load.

The U.S. Lifesaving Service station at Sturgeon Bay, Wisconsin later spotted the schooner flying distress signals and quickly dispatched a rescue team. Despite a sighting during a brief break in the snowstorm, visibility again diminished. The search continued for two hours, but the ship was not seen again.

———

Then there's the disappearance concerning the freighter, the *O. M. McFarland*. The freighter did not disappear, but its captain did!

The ship was coming from Lake Erie loaded with coal. The journey was slow due to the breakup of spring ice, but the freighter was on its last leg heading for Port Washington, Wisconsin. The captain was exhausted from guiding the ship through the ice floes encountered in the Straits of Mackinaw. He retired to his cabin around 10:15 p.m. on April 28, 1937 with instructions to his second mate to wake him as they approached their destination.

About three hours later, the second mate went below to wake the captain. He knocked on the locked door and called out, but there was no answer. He opened the door with a key and entered. The bed was empty. The crew searched the ship thoroughly. Captain George R. Donner was never seen again. He disappeared on his 58th birthday and—at a point and time where the freighter was reported to be near the center of the northwest portion of the *Triangle*.

Planes

One of the most famous airliner disappearances into the *Triangle* occurred on Friday, June 23, 1950 during a raging thunderstorm over Lake Michigan. Northwest #2501 left New York's LaGuardia Airport at 7:30 p.m. en route to Seattle with a scheduled stop at Minneapolis.

Both the captain and the co-pilot were experienced and capable pilots, familiar with the route and the Douglas DC-4 they were flying. The flight plan called for an altitude of 6,000 feet. The captain requested an altitude of 4,000 feet because of the storm, but was denied due to traffic at that altitude. The flight plan was set at 6,000 feet, but reduced to 4,000 near Cleveland. Forty minutes later it was dropped to 3,500 feet to allow sufficient clearance of another plane.

By 11:51 p.m. Eastern Time, the plane entered the storm near Battle Creek, Michigan. As the pilot approached the lake, he requested an altitude adjustment to 2,500 feet (for reasons unknown) but was denied. Just north of Benton Harbor the DC-4 headed out over the lake.

Just before midnight (Central Time) Milwaukee advised that Flight #2501 was missing. At daybreak rescue teams began to search the fog-enshrouded lake.

Neither the aircraft nor any of the 58 people aboard were ever seen again. The Coast Guard did, however, discover a few pieces from the wreckage about twelve miles north of Benton Harbor. Northwest blankets, a logbook, maintenance chart and a few body fragments were found. It was unusual that there was no "debris field" typical of large airline crashes. Nothing else was ever recovered.

On March 20, 1965 a schoolteacher from the Chicago area took off from Wings Airport in Chicago and headed out over Lake Michigan. She had not filed a flight plan, but carried enough fuel for 4-1/2 hours. The Cessna vanished from the Federal Aeronautics Administration radarscope just southwest of Ludington. Neither the pilot nor the plane was ever seen again.

In Sunday, September 9, 2001 another small Cessna airplane, with four people aboard, disappeared in this area. The four, including three licensed pilots, were en route from Dayton, Ohio to Racine, Wisconsin in their rented plane. They were heading home from a visit to Dayton's U.S. Air Force Museum. The plane was last spotted on radar at O'Hare International Airport "shortly after 6 p.m." Coast Guard officials there said the plane was three to five miles east of Wilmette Harbor when it descended from 1,500 feet to 300 feet in less than a minute. The control tower in Elgin Illinois lost contact with the plane at 6:18 p.m. It was one of the last of a series of planes that vanished without a trace into the *Triangle.*

UFOs

At 2 a.m. on June 24, 1950 (coincidentally near to the time that the Coast Guard began its search for missing NW #2501) two policemen north of Milwaukee saw an eerie red glowing object hovering in the east/southeast sky (west of Ludington). They watched it for about 10 minutes, and then it disappeared.

Unidentified flying objects have been reported over the Michigan Triangle since 1897, when Benton Harbor, Michigan residents reported a "huge fire ball" lingering in the sky for nearly 15 minutes. Similar sightings occurred over the next few days near Manitowoc, Wisconsin.

Throughout the years numerous reports have been made of UFOs in the above-mentioned area. One of the most significant, at least in numbers, occurred on March 8, 1994. The following is an excerpt from a report by Dave Reinhart, Bureau of Investigation of Mysteries & Unusual Phenomena in Michigan taken from "The Outer Connection" newsletter. The encounters are documented below (as reported on web site www.qtm.net).

> Several minutes before the 'objects' appeared on the exhibit radar printout, other objects were tracked by sophisticated sites across the United States.
>
> The first group of 24 objects approached the west coast of California from the southwest over the Pacific Ocean and appeared to be on a course toward Lake Michigan.
>
> At about the same time, a group of 14 objects were tracked approaching the southeast from Florida and an additional group of 245 objects approached from over the Alaska and the Northwest Territory of Canada, also appearing to be headed toward Lake Michigan.
>
> Simultaneously a group of 12 objects appeared approaching from the East Coast of the United States coming from the northeast and were observed at Loring AFB.

(Note: Loring Air Force Base is located in Maine.)

All the groups actually converged at a point approximately 52,000 feet above the north central portion of Lake Michigan.

The newsletter goes on to give a transcript of a National Weather Service employee making a 911 call while observing the convergence of the UFOs. Excerpts follow:

> Let me get on closer range....Oh jeez! I'm looking at it in vertical now, and I....
>
> That is a large return down there. Well, it disappeared. But it was up about 6,000 feet...It's moving...I can see it move...
>
> Well, we, we, ah, get the range stroke... Let's see...oh ah...it's gone up...at about 12,000 feet.
>
> Now I'm getting multiple returns. Oh my God! What is this!... It's three and they're lengthwise...They're separated by about 50 km... They're spiking so it's s-s-something pretty solid...It's not precipitation or anything, especially at that height.
>
> I'm seeing three! They look like a triangle on my scope. I'm seeing three of those. They're very strong! These are huge returns. I've never seen anything like this!
>
> They're just popping up all over the place!
>
> They come together and then they separate, and they just keep doing this...

Now I'm getting four...I got four for awhile.
They're all up around um...12000 ft....

Okay, now they've moved position again.
These are bigger than planes!

Another report that evening claims the "objects were
performing comprehensible maneuvers." Still another
describes the event as "a string of Christmas lights up
in the sky." Supposedly over 300 witnesses in 42
Michigan counties as far north as the Upper
Peninsula looked to the sky that night in awe and
amazement.

Three contingents totaling about 50 unidentified
objects converged over the north end of the *Triangle*.
There was no War of the Worlds, no alien assault. But
what was this??? Was it a mock attack by beings from
another universe? It happened just last decade...was
it a practice run for some future transgression?
Something else? Or a very elaborate hoax?

No major incidents have been reported lately in the
Lake Michigan Triangle area, but I have to admit to a
feeling of uneasiness whenever I travel on a
commercial flight and realize that at that moment I
am probably flying somewhere near the center of the
Triangle.

I remarked to my husband that the ferry route looks
like it borders the northern line of that triangle every
day. He remarked, "They probably have a 'Get Across
the Lake Free' card!

CHAPTER 12

SPIRITS WITH A WHITE CAST

**As hollow trees
Are haunts of bees,
For ever going and coming;
So this crystal hive
Is all alive
With a swarming
and buzzing and humming.**[15]

In the mid 1800s a small settlement was established on the western shore of Lake Michigan about 15 miles south of Sturgeon Bay and 30 miles east of Green Bay. The native Potawatomi Indians called the area An-Ne-Pe, "land of the great gray wolf." Spelled *Ahnapee* by immigrant European settlers, the city known today as *Algoma* (another Indian name meaning "park of flowers") grew to become the largest commercial fishing port on the Lake.

The four-story Austrian-style building that housed the Ahnapee Beer Brewery in the mid-19th-century today is home to the von Stiehl Winery. After the brewery closed around 1900, the building was used for storage, as a feed mill and a washing machine facility. Dr. Charles Stiehl purchased the dilapidated old Civil-War-era building in 1964, remodeled it, and moved his burgeoning cherry wine-making business out of his home basement. Wisconsin's oldest winery is now

---

[15] From *Catawba Wine*,"Henry Wadsworth Longfellow

registered in the National Historical Register of Historical Sites.

The von Stiehl Winery, Algoma, Wisconsin.

Dr. Stiehl wrapped his wine bottles in a white "cast," of gauze and plaster of Paris, much like he repaired broken limbs in his medical practice! This covering was designed to protect the beverage from light and temperature changes--and, as an added plus, an extra protection against bottle breakage!

The wine is fermented, aged, and finally bottled in the underground arched limestone caverns dating back to the Civil War. Some bottles are crystal clear; some are cloaked in the cast white. As in Longfellow's "crystal hive" there is much activity involved at von Stiehls in the production of their well-known Door County cherry wine, their famed German Riesling, and over two dozen other favorites including Apple Icing and Oktoberfest, both gold-medal winners at the 2012 WI State Fair Professional Wine Competition.

Henry Schmiling was the original brew master here (and, it seems, continues to be the phantom of the winery!) In 1981 his son, Bill, and daughter-in-law, Sandy, took over the business. Today the winery is owned by third-generation—sons Aric and Brad.

Shaun Schmiling, Brad's wife, is a teacher at Oconto Falls and Southern Door. She began working at the winery in1999. Shaun says a lot of mysterious things occur here. Lights come on after being turned off. Doors open by themselves. Things are moved around. Dogs whimper and appear to be very nervous inside the building.

Shaun admitted to having some doubts about her memory when strange things began to happen, but then started paying closer attention to details. She relates, "We would come into work in the morning and find bricks lying in the middle of the floor right inside the door," certain that they were not there when she closed the shop the previous night and with no clue as to where they came from.

At one point in time winery employees had to wash down all the floors in the cellar. After cleaning the floors of all debris, but before washing them, the workers discovered a piece of paper lying on the dry floor. It was a receipt signed by one of the family many years ago, back when the building was a feed mill!

Supposedly, there was an extensive tunnel system under the city of Algoma, originally designed to move coal off and distribute it from the ore boats. Years ago "we were going to see if we could extend our tunnels," Shaun recalls. An employee was assigned to punch a hole in the wall to see what was on the other side. He found sand. The workers then left for lunch. When they came back, the tools were standing on end blocking part of the walkway in front of the tunnel. Some time later they left the work area again. When they came back, the tools were standing on end again, but now they were blocking the door to the complete area. The next morning there was a cross of seven stones in front of the hole that had been made in the wall. A member of the clergy was called in to bless the building.

Sandy Schmiling, describes herself as "a pragmatic type personality." She claims to be a "believer," but has no ghost stories of "her own." She does, however, relate examples of incidents experienced by her husband and other family members. And she believes that the resident ghost is a "friendly" phantom.

"Bill's sister, who worked here years ago, had many experiences" with lights and noises. Sandy explained that her sister-in-law "was into the occult and taro cards" and probably was more in tune with supernatural experiences. Son Aric has mentioned to his mom that "things sometimes change location when he visits the winery at night."

Despite the fact that the ghost occupies a building brimming with fine *wines*, he seems to prefer *beer!* Sandy recalls that Bill was working late at night going up and down the stairs between the four floors. As he was going *up* the steps he saw an open can of beer on the stairs that wasn't there when he went *down*. This happened several times.

Case-club members were invited to semi-annual five-course catered dinners in the galleria. Henry used to be present at the dinners as well. "Maybe we are taking his space, Sandy mused. "He stopped after the first few times."

On March 22, 2002 a team of four ghost hunters from Wisconsin Area Ghost Investigations out of central Wisconsin spent about three hours here. They reported significant temperature drops at various locations throughout the building, including a decrease in the lobby of 14.1 degrees within nine minutes. Their equipment recorded a temperature decrease of nearly 20 degrees on the 2nd level and a drop of 14.6 degrees on the 4th level. It has been surmised that quick temperature drops (or sometimes rises) may be an indication of ghost energy. Orbs appeared in some photos taken by the group, leading them to believe there are at least two spirits that haunt the winery. Orbs, circular translucent spots appearing on a photograph but not seen by the human eye, are believed to be a spirit form of some sort. Spirit lights are often seen by the human eye in the form of a white streak passing through space. (I believe that I may have seen a spirit light the night I spent at the Historic Karsten Inn!)

The group believes there is a male ghost here (Henry) but that there may be one or more additional ghosts— perhaps female. The group speculates that (due to the proximity of the winery to Lake Michigan) perhaps "she" drowned in the Lake or had some connection with the shipping industry years ago.

An employee at the winery, Edye Urban (see Chapters 5 and 6) gives tours and hosts wine tasting. Edye told me of a man (who we will call Jim) who toured the winery with his mother a few years ago and related the following story to her.

Jim worked at von Stiehl's over twenty years ago. On his last day at the winery, he was giving a tour as well as relating stories about Henry. When he looked up to the fourth-floor window, Jim saw a man with a big top hat looking down at him. He recalled that there were only two guys working that day: one in the tasting room and one as tour guide. After finishing with his tour, Jim unlocked the door to the fourth-floor storage room and peered in; nobody was there.

Edye recalled one day when she was serving samples of wine to a couple of young women who were carrying on a conversation.

> One of them said, 'I understand this place is haunted.' All of a sudden, the top from the wine decanter flips off the decanter and lands in the garbage can four or five feet away. This has happened a few times. The glass decanter is only partially full, yet occasionally flips its lid!

I returned to the winery a year after my first visit. Edye was working that day. I also met with the winery manager, Sallie Marquart, and employee Karen Vanderhoof.

Sallie serves up wine samples along with
employees Edye (center) and Karen (left).

Sallie was hired in June 2006. Her father had worked here years ago with Dr. Stiehl. A little less than a week after she was hired, employees found rocks in three places on the main floor…small piles of gray cement that could not have chipped off and fallen from the painted white brick in the room. Sallie had closed up the building the night before and knew the floor was clean when she left. The staff has told Sallie rocks show up on the floor every now and then, and nobody can figure out where they come from.

Sallie talked of another incident that happened one day when she "was going to help the guys bottle" the wine. She wore jeans and a tee shirt to work and brought a change of clothes along in her brief case. When she finished working in the cellar, she opened her brief case. Her jersey skirt was there, but not the top. "I thought it must have fallen out of my brief case," Sallie recalled. She checked her car; it wasn't there. In fact, the jersey shirt did not reappear until three weeks later. Sallie was going through a storage room upstairs. There, in the middle of the pink-carpeted floor, was her green shirt!

Sallie took me into the cellar. We walked down the first set of stairs, turned to the left and were walking to the second set of stairs when I heard someone walk down the stairs behind us. I turned around to look, but nobody rounded the corner and I didn't hear anyone go back up the stairs. I got involved in another conversation when we came back to the main floor and forgot about the incident. So I e-mailed Sallie and asked if either of the two employees working that day had come down the stairs right after us. Here's her response: "It wasn't Karen or Edye, but we couldn't remember if a customer was going upstairs to the galerie or not. So…who knows?! LOL." I remember that there were very few people in the building at the time. The sound (of the steps) was clear and rapid, but, like Sallie says, "who knows?!"

The winery restrooms seem to be hot spots for mysterious activities. Every evening before closing, employees prop open the doors. One evening a wastebasket used to hold it open was moved, and the door was shut. Another morning Sallie walked into the men's room and found a picture on the floor propped up against the wall. "Did you hear anything drop on the floor?" she asked the other two gals working that morning. Nobody had. The night before, as the two were preparing to lock up the building, Sallie caught a fleeting glance of a man on the other side of the open bathroom door. Thinking someone might still be in the building, the women checked out the room. Nothing was amiss; nobody was in the bathroom. "It was probably Henry," Sallie recalls as she dismisses the incidents!

Edye talks of things that go boom in the women's bathroom. One woman put her purse on the table in the room. While she was sitting there, the purse flew off the table onto the floor, spilling all of its contents. Another woman felt a presence in the room. Then a book fell off the table and she heard a scraping sound. Then "I got out," the woman said, still fastening her slacks as she hurriedly exited the room! Still another woman heard "papers scraping across the floor" and other strange noises in the room.

Keys disappear. Sallie looked for a set of spare keys that she kept in a storage drawer. Later she found the keys in an extra pair of shoes she keeps at the winery!

Cases of wine just fall over, corks shoot across the room, lights turn on and off by themselves. Karen has experienced the lights dimming many times and frequently feels a presence in the room.

A lady touring the winery in 2006 revealed that she was with the Southern Paranormal Research Group. During the tour she felt the presence of a spirit in the galerie. She believes that there may be three ghosts in the building. At this time, however, only one seems to reveal himself. As HENRY Wadsworth Longfellow wrote phrases of the "Song of the Vine," I can picture HENRY Schmiling smiling from the upstairs window, while quoting Longfellow's praises of the premium Door-County cherry wines he has made so popular.

While pure as a spring
Is the wine I sing
And to praise it, one needs but name it;
For (*our cherry*) wine
Has need of no sign,
No tavern-bush to proclaim it.[16]

Sallie Marquardt points to
a showcase of fine wines.

---

[16] From *Catawba Wine*, Henry Wadsworth Longfellow

For reasons I won't go into here, this book has taken a bit of time from start to finish. As a final step, I decided to check back at a few of my favorite haunts to see if anything noteworthy was happening since I had last visited. It appears that Henry, and maybe other ghosts, still delight the folks at the winery.

Edye Urban related that she was helping to prepare for an upcoming Murder Mystery dinner. A couple of days before the event, she was cleaning in the very back of the lower level tunnel system. After sweeping and vacuuming, Edye started to mop the floors. About half way through her job, Edye heard a dinner bell ring in the area she was in. She looked around, went in an adjoining room...there were no bells. "Well Henry," Edye flippantly addressed the spirit that resides in the cellar, "I'm a little hard of hearing. If you want to have dinner with me, you will have to ring the bell louder!" She excitedly added, "He heard me." The bell immediately rang in a very loud tone!

The non-profit Fox Valley Ghost Hunters out of the Appleton, Wisconsin area recently visited the winery. I spoke with Craig Nehring, head of the group. He confirmed that Henry seems to like the cellar area, but he claims another phantom he calls Christopher spends time in the office on the top floor. Their photographic equipment caught an elongated shadow, perhaps a tall man, go out the exit and then dart back in. The words "what" and "no" were heard from their voice recorder.

The winery has a production area in an old warehouse across the street. Craig went on to tell of their experiences there. "The warehouse is crazy. One investigator got possessed with negative energy. She started barking orders at us." Craig went on to say that they then "saged" her. The term describes an American Indian procedure of smudging burned dried herbs, such as sage, onto the victim. The smoke carries the negative energy into another space where it is released and purified. A member of the group said a prayer over the possessed woman.

When she returned to her normal "down-to-earth" self, the investigator told the group of her weird vision. Craig continued, "She was to take all of us out to the lighthouse (in Algoma) and drown us."

Craig Nehring of FVGH

The group believes that the warehouse used to be a brothel, in the early to mid-twentieth century. Craig described their investigation.

> Each bedroom has a door going in one side and out the other, and there are two staircases in the front and back of the building. We picked up weird voices, sexually oriented. Each of our members took a different room. I was in the blue room. It had one shelf, and a light bulb hanging down from the ceiling. I heard a noise, like a

squeaky board. I then asked out loud, "Am I making you mad?"

Just then the door slammed shut, missing his shoulder by inches. Craig opened the door, but he "couldn't recreate the scenario; the door wanted to stay open." There was even a hole in the wall where it seemed to rest. Five minutes later he got on his voice recorder and asked "Any chance you could make this happen again?" An answer came back: "Nope."

Down the hall from where the door slammed, a similar light bulb on a cord started to swing wildly back and forth. The group had walkie-talkies on them. They had left a set downstairs. A voice from the empty downstairs room was heard: "Do you agree?"

What is agreed, among employees, ghost hunters, and many visitors to the winery, is that strange things continue to happen at both the winery and the production area, and Henry Schmilling *stiehl* roams the premises--and probably has some spirited company!

CHAPTER 13

THE HAUNTED FARMHOUSE

**I never have seen a haunted house,
But I hear there are such things;
That they hold the talk of spirits,
Their mirth and sorrowings.**[17]

I picked up the phone and answered it in my usual manner, giving our business name and then my first name. The voice on the other end asked excitedly, "Are you a ghost buster?" I answered that I was not, but told the lady that I was a writer of ghost stories. "Well," exclaimed the voice, "I have one for YOU."

Twenty-year-old Mallory Williams, along with husband Brad, Brad's mother, and the couple's two small children moved into an old farmhouse on Shiloh Road. This is just inside Sturgeon Bay city limits and just under two miles from the point where Highways 42/57 cross the Sturgeon Bay Ship Canal and head northeast into Wisconsin's Upper Door County—a well-known tourist destination with its great restaurants, quaint little shops, varied recreational opportunities...and, of course, cherries!

It was the day after Halloween in the fall of 2006 when the Williams moved into their rented farmhouse. Mallory described that she felt "an uneasiness, a creepy feeling" but didn't mention it to her family. Maybe it was just the empty building and the gloomy

---

[17] From *The House With Nobody In It*, Joyce Kilmer

autumn day. In fact, after a long day moving all of their belongings, Mallory remembers having no trouble falling sleep that evening, no unusual activities. All went well; everything was fine...for a couple of days!

Then things began to happen during the nighttime hours. Someone—or at least that someone's footsteps—would follow Mallory up the stairs. All night long the family would hear the footsteps going up and down the stairs.

The family would find light bulbs unscrewed in the basement. Occasionally all the lights in the house would go out. Mallory went on. "We couldn't figure out why the circuit breaker would have an overload because nothing had changed; we didn't plug anything else in or do anything to cause this." After one such "blackout," Mallory's mother-in-law shouted "Knock it off and behave." Things were fine again...for a while!

"Someone" began unplugging the heater in the bedroom. Blankets in son Aiden's room would be pulled from his crib and left lying on the floor. Mallory's favorite blanket disappeared. The next day she was showing a friend around the house and telling her about the missing blanket. After walking into Aiden's room the friend spotted the blanket rolled into a tight ball and placed behind the nursery cart! Mallory believes the ghost might be a child. "It seems to like Aiden's room the best—and it seems to have an obsession with blankets!"

Things started to bump or thump in the night! The family cat hears the noises too. Mallory knows this because "sometimes the cat's hair will stand on end, it's back arched and hissing."

Then the incidents started to happen during the daytime too. Mallory's aunt visited her one afternoon about three weeks after they had moved in. They both heard the sound of footsteps following them down the stairs...twice! The TV started to turn itself off, or get fuzzy for no apparent reason, and "someone" rearranged the silverware drawer while everyone was seated around the kitchen table!

Mallory discovered that her friend, Susan, had rented a room in this very same farmhouse a couple of years ago. She too, claimed the sound of footsteps followed her up the stairs. Mallory spoke with the landlord— who "was not very helpful with information." But, yet, there seemed to be some reticence, perhaps something that her landlord did not want to talk about. The incidents continued.

I did not hear from Mallory for a long period of time. When I tried to phone her at the farmhouse, I found her family had moved. I finally reached her at her place of employment. Although she did not seem pressured to cut the conversation short, I nevertheless sensed a slight curtness, a reluctance to talk about her experiences. Mallory said she would call me back soon. I understood that she probably could not talk freely at that time. I had called her at work because I could not find another phone number, and to ask her to return my call at her convenience. I never heard from Mallory again.

She seemed so eager to talk that first day she contacted me. She promised me she would gather more information and send me a few pictures. Now it was like she wanted anonymity. So we will give Mallory and her family that. I have changed her name and those of her family members in this story.

But I can't help but wonder what drove the family to move out of a house that they had only lived in for a few short months. Sometimes I think about Mallory, and I wonder who lives in the farmhouse now, and if they are experiencing any psychic occurrences. Maybe someday I will investigate further. But for now...I will let sleeping phantoms lie!

Note: When I finished writing this chapter, I decided to review another chapter that appears earlier in the book. When I was into that chapter, I hit the "PgDn" key on my keyboard and what should appear but the first page of "The Haunted Farmhouse" chapter! Confused, I paged up to see if I had mistakenly erased something in the other chapter. I went back to where I had been. Nothing had changed. "The Haunted Farmhouse" was back where it should have been! Is the Farmhouse Phantom playing with me????!

CHAPTER 14

DOGMAN DOGMA

**Somewhere in the northwoods darkness
A creature walks upright
And the best advice you may ever get
Is don't go out at night.**[18]

It seems only fitting that since we started this book with a story of werewolves, that we finish with one on Bigfoot, or as they say in the upper part of lower Michigan...dogman!! (I have often wondered why these creatures are never referred to in the plural as dogmen, or Bigfeet or sasquatches; the plural of werewolf is werewolves.)

Bigfoot, or sasquatch as he is sometimes known, has been spotted throughout the United States over the years—probably more frequently in forests of the Pacific Northwest. Tales were told by Native American Indians of dark and hairy creatures about eight feet tall that wander through the forests and often emit horrible screams at night.

Wayne King, of the Michigan/Canadian Bigfoot Information Center located southeast of Bay City, claims to have seen three of the scary creatures. He has been tracking the animals since 1970. King was taken aback with their large glowing bright white eyes that he describes as "the size of golf balls."

---

[18] From *The Legend*, Steve Cook

There are those who say we cannot prove that Bigfoot exists until one is hunted and killed. Wayne King is out to fulfill that premise. He carries a rifle in the woods and admits having one in his sights once, but because he could not see the large glaring eyes, decided against shooting it. King says that he has been warned by the Department of Natural Resources that he could be prosecuted if or when he kills a Bigfoot...or dogman. (However, other accounts say that the DNR claims never to have heard of Wayne King.)

Steve Cook, the production director for WTCM in Traverse City, Michigan, wrote the lyrics to *The Legend* as an April Fool's joke in 1987, making most of it up strictly from his imagination. The song told of such a creature that "walked like men and screamed"...and killed! After *The Legend* was played on the local radio, stories started to pour in about sightings of just such a "dogman." As a result the song became the most requested on WTCM! As most novelties, however, it soon died out and was removed from the play list...until the Luther incident (read on)! After that, requests for the song poured in from all over the U.S. (and a couple of foreign countries). Cook, who had destroyed the original master tape, returned to the studio to record a new version with an added verse.

Many sightings have occurred in and near the Manistee National Forest just east of Lake Michigan, running from just north of Muskegon all the way up to near Traverse City.

Luther Looter

Several paw prints were found surrounding a remote cabin near Luther (southwest of Cadillac, Michigan) in July 1987. Deep cuts and teeth marks were found around doors and windows to the cabin, and screens were ripped apart. An article about a convincingly credible creature that may have vandalized the cabin appeared in the *Cadillac Evening News* and in the *Grand Rapids Press*. From there, newspapers across the U.S. (including *U.S.A. Today*) picked up the story over the Associated Press newswire. Paul Harvey announced the incident on one of his daily broadcasts. Then, Steve Cook added another verse to T*he Legend.*

In the summer of '87,
near Luther it happened again.
At a cabin in the woods, It looked like
maybe someone had tried to break in.
There were cuts in the door that could only have
been made by very sharp teeth and claws.
He didn't wear shoes 'cause he didn't have feet;
He walked on just two paws.[19]

Five hundred copies of the updated song sold out in less than twelve days.

Interlochen Encounter

Veronica Freels was taking her daughter home from a concert at the Interlochen Academy of Arts in July of 1997. Deciding to try a shortcut home, she became lost in a wooded area. The road she had chosen turned from a paved county road into a gravel trail that narrowed down into a logging or hunting road with evergreen trees and bushes scraping against her car.

As she began to back up, her daughter, Amanda, screamed and pointed to an object ahead of the car. Veronica relates that the animal that was walking

---

[19] From *The Legend*, Steve Cook

slowly down the road into the forest. "It was on two legs, very tall, but hunched over." As she brightened the car lights, the creature turned its head to look at the women. "It was covered in thick black hair. The eyes reflected the light, just like a raccoon or a dog's eyes would."

Months later, when Veronica listed to "The Legend" on WTCM, she knew what she had seen that summer was indeed the "Dogman."

Midnight Madness

A government official, who wishes to remain anonymous, was headed back to his home in Traverse City. He had spent the evening at a friend's house in Benzonia and was traveling down Cinder Road a few miles from Bendon. It was about midnight when his headlights picked up a reflection from an animal's eyes. Thinking it was a deer, the man slowed down as he approached the roadside figure. As he came closer, he realized that it was something else! A dark, hairy creature, about six feet tall, was standing over a deer road kill. As he brought his truck to a stop, he got a better look at this animal that was still standing over the deer, but now it was staring back at him!

For a moment, he believed someone was playing some kind of joke using a large stuffed animal. It would be highly unlikely to be able to get so close were it a live wild animal! But just as these thoughts were racing through his head, the creature dropped to all four legs and ran across the road and into the woods. As one who hunted bear every year, he knew that it was "absolutely not"" the carnivore (or omnivore if you choose) that regularly inhabits the Michigan wilds! He added, "No, whatever that was, it was for real."

Within a few moments realization as to what had just happened sunk in. The man hesitantly grabbed a flashlight and his digital camera from his glove compartment and cautiously crossed the road, keeping in mind that he could quickly get back to the open truck door in about three or four steps!

Luckily, the soil was soft next to the road and there were a few good paw prints appearing to be seven or eight inches long! He was able to snap a couple of good pictures, one using a spent shotgun shell to illustrate the enormity of the prints!

If nobody else believes the pictures, at least he will always remember that this was NOT a dream!

Gable Film

In the fall of 1997 a 3-1/2 minute 8mm film was found in an old box at an estate sale. The movie was believed to have been taken sometime in the 1970s. At the very end of the film there appeared an image looking much like the dogman described in *The Legend*.

It was ten years later when Steve Cook first introduced the Gable film on his website, describing it as an amateur attempt to produce a movie that was probably never intended for broad distribution. His website was hacked, the film and other files stolen and posted on the web as an "Intentional Hoax." The film generated a great deal of interest, however. Even after it disappeared from the internet, many requests came in to review and enhance the old film. The study produced some interesting findings.

The first frames focus on a creature sitting on the forest floor with an outstretched leg about 50 yards from the cameraman. Though dark and with pointed ears, the broad-shouldered image resembles a human in some aspects. It starts to move in what is described as a "commando-style crawl." Suddenly it lunges toward the camera on all fours, looking more like a large black dog with a tail swinging as it runs. The last frame shows the creature charging toward the cameraman with all four feet off the ground—a movement deemed impossible for humans!

The film was digitally duplicated to the highest resolution, bringing out details and reduced to individual images. The enhanced pictures show the creature's eyes, ears, snout and what looks like an extended lower jaw.

Reed City Sighting

Sightings had been reported in 2006 near a vacant building just outside of Reed City. A college student from Big Rapids convinced three of his buddies to check out the story. They arrived at the building about 2:30 a.m. and waited quietly in their car. About a half hour later, they saw movement in the nearby woods and heard the sound of twigs breaking. The creature, described by the student as "NOT human...NOT natural...and NOT friendly", seemed to be hiding and peering out from behind a tree. The headlights from the car returned a "yellow glow" reflected from its eyes.

Frightened, the boys left the area. But after boosting each other's bravado, they turned the car around and returned to their original parking site. Searching the area with their flashlights, the group suddenly heard a rustling noise and a motion sensor light went on near the vacant building. Once again, they tore away from the area. As they looked behind them, the creature was chasing them, running along behind the car on all fours!

The Eye

A hunter, walking his property in Antrim County in early January 2007, placed a motion-sensitive digital camera on a platform mounted in a tree to monitor deer and small game. The camera was originally placed too low, gathering pictures of a few squirrels and a lot of blowing leaves! The camera lens was then mounted about six feet above the ground, producing pictures of white tail deer—until one day when he discovered the camera had been knocked from the platform and was dangling by its cord.

After downloading the latest pictures into his camera, he found three amazing images: of a human looking eye that appears to protrude from a hairy face, some crooked teeth and a furry foot! The image of the teeth appears to have been taken just as the camera was falling from its platform. It shows a snout with canine-looking teeth. The third image seems to have caught a dangling shot of a furry paw standing on a deer leg stripped to the bone. No remains were found at the site.

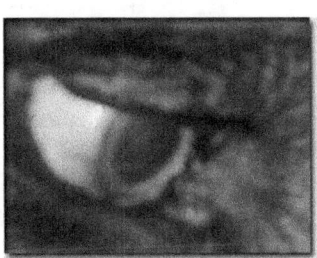

Dangling Digital Camera in woods "shoots" an eyeful!
(Photo from www.michigan-dogman.com)

Sightings of the Dogman in Michigan have dwindled in the past several months.

**So far this spring
No stories have appeared.
Have the dogmen gone away?
Have they disappeared?**[13]

Let us take pause here (pun intended) and remember, however, that if you think about taking a walk after dark in or near the Manistee National Forest:

**Somewhere in the northwoods darkness
A creature walks upright
The best advice you may ever get
Is don't go out at night!**[20]

---

[20] Steve Cook, *The Legend*

CHAPTER 15

DON'T GIVE UP THE GHOST

**Frigid white winter,
Wilted brown oak leaves still cling;
They won't give up the ghost.**[21]

Like oak leaves cling to the tree waiting for another season to finally move on to their resting place, some spirits seem to cling to the familiar places they know and love. Some of these spirits seem to have unfinished business there or need permission to move on. Whatever their reason, they seem to linger in a different plane of time, energy and space.

The preceding tales are only a tip of the supernatural iceberg. If you are interested in discovering stories of your own (and having a fascinating time doing so), spend the night at a haunted hotel or bed-and-breakfast establishment, or visit an old lighthouse and talk with the guides and volunteers. Question friends and people that you meet; you are sure to get a story or two that piques your interest! You might even find persons with psychic capabilities and amazing real-life experiences of their own.

A few "Don't Miss" haunted places to visit in Wisconsin/Michigan are The Historic Karsten Inn (now the Kewaunee Inn) in downtown Kewaunee, Wisconsin (spend the night in Room 310); the Seul Choix lighthouse near Gulliver, Michigan (watch the

---

[21] "Demise," Enid Cleaves

videos in the gift shop area); and the Paulding Light north of Watersmeet, Michigan (the nightly show starts at dusk). Of course, there are many more; visit some of those that I have written about...or check out an unlimited number of sources on the internet.

I continue to enjoy my experiences that cause me to wonder, and revel in the stories told by reliable and respected people that I know and trust. I look for new places to visit and explore. Recently I accompanied members of the FVGH in a flashlight tour of a vacant, rundown Catholic church in Berlin, Wisconsin; next on my list is to go through the old tannery there. I've witnessed some questionable incidences, for sure. I would love to see a materialization, and I am not about to "give up the ghost!"

May the good spirits be with you!

SELECTED BIBLIOGRAPHY

Articles, Books and Newspapers

Giles, Diane. "Christmas Tree Ship Named After Longtime Kenosha Resident," *Kenosha News,* January 1, 2008.

Great Lakes Atlas, Environment Canada and U. S. Environmental Protection Agency, 1995.

Hollatz, Tom. *Gangster Holidays, the Lore and Legends of the Bad Guys.* North Star Press of St. Cloud Inc., 2005.

Mality, Abner (i.e.; Dr. Abner Mality). "Wisconsin Werewolf," *Wormwood Chronicals.*

Mason, Kathy S. "Mystery at Sand Point Lighthouse," *Michigan History* (Sept./Oct. 2003): 21-27

Skubal, Michael. "Depp Movie to be Filmed in Northwoods," *Rhinelander Daily News,* February 6, 2008.

Stonehouse, Frederick. *Haunted Lakes II.* Duluth: Lake Superior Port Cities Inc., 2000.

Urbank, Vicki. "Alice Gray, Woman of the Dunes," *Chicago Examiner,* July 1916.

Interviews

Barr, Jim. Volunteer, Seul Choix Lighthouse, Gulliver, MI (7/05/05).

Hayden, Don. Kewaunee, WI (11/26/04).

Lockhart, Maudie. Volunteer, Seul Choix Lighthouse, Gulliver, MI (7/05/05).

Lundin, Betty. Volunteer, Sand Point Lighthouse, Escanaba, MI (9/04).

Marquardt, Sallie. Manager, von Stiehl Winery, Algoma, WI (11/05/06)
Nerby, Lawrence. Neighbor, Manitowish Waters, WI (5/08).

1

Raychel, Ray. Mt. Morris, WI (6/05).

Schmiling, Sandra and Shaun. von Stiehl Winery, Algoma, WI (11/25/05).

Schuller, Tom. President, Kewaunee, WI Area Historical Society (11/27/04).

Urban, Edith. Casco, Wisconsin (11/26/04).

Wagner, Jerry. Manitowish Waters, WI (5/06/08).

Williams, Mallory. Sturgeon Bay, WI (12/06).

Web Sites

Algoma Chamber of Commerce, www.algoma.org

"Alice Gray, Woman of the Dunes," Vicki Uranik. www.chestertontribune.com

"Alpena Goes Missing," www.michiganshipwrecks.org

"Bigfoot is Out There," www.petoskeynews.com/ articles/2005/10/28/features/outdoors

"The Biograph Theater—The Life & Mysterious Death of John Dillinger, 2433 North Lincoln Avenue," www.prairieghosts.com/dillinger

"The Bray Road Beast," www.prairieghosts.com

"Captain Joseph W. Townshend and the Seul Choix Point Lighthouse," Jan Langley. www.lighthousedepot.com

"Cessna Disappears in the Lake Michigan Triangle," www.mimufon.org

"Chesterton – Diana of the Dunes," www.theshadowlands.net/places/indiana

"Classic Michigan Cases: From Michigan MUFON-" www.members.tripod.com

"The Contributions of Women to the United States Naval Observatory: The Early Years." www.maia.usno.navy.mil/women_history/gray

II

"The Dillinger Gang," www.geocities.com

"John Dillinger: Bank Robber or Robin Hood," www.crimelibrary.com/gangsters_outlaws

"The Disappearance of Flight 2501," www.michiganshipwrecksorg

"Exit the Wolfman: Gable Film Update," www.cryptomundo.com/cryptozoo-news/exit-wolfman

"The Fate of the Christmas Tree Ship," www.epa.gov/glnpo/monitoring/great_minds_great lakes/history/ghristmastree.html

"Ghost Road," www.indianaghosts.homestead.com

"Ghost Stories Draw Tourists to Lighthouse," www.thehollandsentinal.net/stories/071199/new

"The Greek Goddess Artemis," www.goddessgift.com/goddess-myths_artemis.htm

"Indiana Ghost Trackers," www.indianaghosts.org/ghoststories

"Inn History of The Kewaunee Inn Property," www.kewauneeinn.com

"Island of Legend," Gerry Volgenau, 2000 www.freep.com/fetures/travel/mani27-20000827.htm

"The Keeper of Seul Choix Point," Ken Rudine. www.texasescapes.com

"Lake Leelanau," www.theshadowlands.net/serpent2

"A Lake Michigan Madcap," Charles E. Brown 1942. www.weird-wi.com/lakes/brown13/htm

"Last Call for Northwest 2501 (1950)" from *UFO Roundup* edited by Joseph Trainor, www.weird-wi.com/weirdstories/2501

"The Legend of Michigan's Dogman," www.michigan-dogman.com/encounters-1997

"Maps and Directions," www.mappoint.msn.com

"Mary Terry, Keeper of the Lighthouse at Escanaba, MIin the Upper Peninsula," www.exploringthenorth.com/sandpoint/maryt

"Michigan Facts," www.wtht.com/pages/michfacts

"Michigan's Fossil Whales," www.sentex.net

"The Michigan Triangle," www.en.wikipedia.org

"'Michigan Triangle' to Blame for Weird Occurrences?" Bill Wangemann, ww.rense.com/general63/mich.htm

"Non-Existent Documents Discovered!" Dave Reinhart www.qtm.net

"Radar Spots 'Ghost Planes" Lake Michigan Triangle," www.ufowisconsin.com/wfiles/files/trghostplanes

"Seeing the Light—Sand Point Lighthouse," www.terrypepper.com/lights/michigan/sandpoint

_____ "Seeing the Light—Seul Choix Light

"A Short Note—John Dillinger," www.home.swipnet.se/roland/dillinger

"Superstitious Warnings and Ghost Ship Sightings," www.christmastreeshipbooks.com

"Tracking Down 'The Beast of Bray Road," www.weird-wi.com

"Types of Sea Serpents," www.theshadowlands.com

"U. S. Navy captures Lake Michigan Monster" www.weeklyworldnews.com

"UFO Updates," UFO Roundup Vol. 7 No. 1,

www.virtually strange.net/ufo/updates/2002

"UFOs, Manitowoc Go Way Back," Rob Bignell,
www.ufowisconsin.com/wfiles/files/Imlakemichigan"

_____ The W-Files," Jay Wrath

von Stiehl Winery, www.vonstiehl.com

"Werewolves in Wisconsin," www.prairieghosts.com

"Werewolves: The Myths and The Truths,"
http:/members.tripod.com

"Where is Joan Williams," www.mimufon.org

"Where the Legend of Sleeping Bear Lives,"
http://home.nycap.rr.cm/ddding/bear.html

"Women of the Light," *Lighthouse Digest,*" Jeremy
D'Entremont . www.foghornpublishing.com

Poems, Songs

Coleridge, Samuel Taylor. "The Rime of the Ancient
Mariner." 1798.

Cleaves, Enid. "Demise," 2009.

Cook, Steve, "The Legend," Mindstage Productions/Ron
Rose Studios. 1987

Gilbert, V. C. (lyrics), Hadler, Mary M. (music) "The Shifting
Whispering Sands," Gallatin Music Corp. 1950.

Eagles, "Hotel California," 1976.

Kilmer, Joyce. "The House With Nobody In It." 1914.

Longfellow, Henry Wadsworth. "The Lighthouse." 1849.

_____ "Catawba Wine." 1854.

Lord Byron, "Solitude."

Poe, Edgar Allan, "A Dream Within a Dream." 1849.

_____ "Spirits of the Dead," 1827.

V

Poem found on building near Biograph Theater a day or two after the shooting of John Dillinger: Author Unknown.1934.

Sandlin Jr., Robert W., "Blood Moon." 2007.

Verse from "The Wolf Man," Universal Pictures, 1941.

Museums and Miscellaneous

Guest room logs at The Historic Karsten Hotel, Kewaunee, Wisconsin, 2004.

The International Wolf Center, Ely, Minnesota.

Sand Point Lighthouse, Escanaba, Michigan.

Seul Choix Point Lighthouse, Gulliver, Michigan.

Video: "True Lighthouse Hauntings," Keweenaw Video Productions of Houghton, Michigan, Frederick Stonehouse, author.

Slide Presentation: "Gangsters of the Northwoods," Mercer, WI Community Center. Presented by students of the Mercer Environmental Tourism Charter School and sponsored by the Mercer Education Foundation. (10/08)